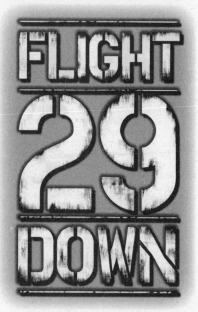

Ten Rules

Stan Rogow Productions · Grosset & Dunlap

GROSSET & DUNLAP
Published by the Penguin Group
Penguin Group (USA) Inc., 375 Hudson Street, New York, New York 10014, U.S.A.
Penguin Group (Canada), 90 Eglinton Avenue East, Suite 700, Toronto, Ontario, Canada M4P 2Y3
(a division of Pearson Penguin Canada Inc.)
Penguin Books Ltd, 80 Strand, London WC2R 0RL, England
Penguin Ireland, 25 St Stephen's Green, Dublin 2, Ireland
(a division of Penguin Books Ltd)
Penguin Group (Australia), 250 Camberwell Road, Camberwell, Victoria 3124, Australia
(a division of Pearson Australia Group Pty Ltd)
Penguin Books India Pvt Ltd, 11 Community Centre, Panchsheel Park, New Delhi - 110 017, India
Penguin Group (NZ), Cnr Airborne and Rosedale Roads, Albany, Auckland 1310, New Zealand
(a division of Pearson New Zealand Ltd)
Penguin Books (South Africa) (Pty) Ltd, 24 Sturdee Avenue, Rosebank, Johannesburg 2196, South Africa

Penguin Books Ltd, Registered Offices:
80 Strand, London WC2R 0RL, England

If you purchased this book without a cover, you should be aware that this book is stolen property.
It was reported as "unsold and destroyed" to the publisher, and neither the author
nor the publisher has received any payment for this "stripped book."

The scanning, uploading, and distribution of this book via the Internet or via any other means without
the permission of the publisher is illegal and punishable by law. Please purchase only authorized
electronic editions, and do not participate in or encourage electronic piracy of copyrighted materials.
Your support of the authors' rights is appreciated.

The publisher does not have any control over and does not assume any responsibility
for author or third-party websites or their content.

Copyright © 2006 Independent Television Project. All rights reserved.

Published by Grosset & Dunlap, a division of Penguin Young Readers Group,
345 Hudson Street, New York, New York 10014. GROSSET & DUNLAP is a trademark
of Penguin Group (USA) Inc. Printed in the U.S.A.

Library of Congress Cataloging-in-Publication Data

Sorrells, Walter.
Ten rules : a novelization / by Walter Sorrells.
p. cm. -- (Flight 29 down)
"Adapted from the teleplays by D.J. MacHale. Based on the TV series
created by D.J. MacHale, Stan Rogow."
ISBN 0-448-44402-X (pbk)
I. MacHale, D. J. II. Rogow, Stan. III. Stan Rogow Productions. IV. Title. V. Series.
PZ7.S9166Tdn 2006
[Fic]--dc22
2006007624

10 9 8 7 6 5 4 3 2 1

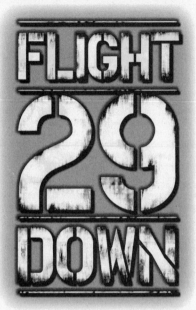

Ten Rules

A novelization by
Walter Sorrells
Adapted from the
teleplays by D.J. MacHale

Based on the
TV series created by
D.J. MacHale
Stan Rogow

Stan Rogow Productions · Grosset & Dunlap

To Molly Kempf—
my inspiration, my muse,
my siren, my everything. —W.S.

PROLOGUE

Dan Rosenthal pulled his car into the driveway of the Hartwell School, an exclusive private school in a suburb of Los Angeles. Rosenthal, the Department of Social Services caseworker for a juvenile ward of the state named Cody Jackson, steered toward a striking modern building at the end of the driveway.

At the entrance to the building, he pulled up on top of a yellow-painted stripe that said NO PARKING, jumped out, and ran into the building.

The place was curiously quiet for a school. *You expect kids to be making a big racket,* thought Rosenthal. A small, plump woman sat behind a counter in the front office. She didn't look up immediately, so he tapped rapidly on the little bell on the counter.

"Hello! Hello! Excuse me!" he said. "*Hello!*"

The plump woman looked up grudgingly. "Yes?"

"Dan Rosenthal, CDSS." He held up his badge. The woman didn't show any sign of being real impressed. "I need a student by the name of Jackson. Cody Jackson."

She looked at him as though there were something about him that vaguely offended her.

"Maybe you'd better speak with Dr. Shook, our headmaster," she said, after she'd finished giving him the stink-eye.

"I don't care about Dr. Whoever, I just need Cody Jackson. Now." He took out his paperwork and set it on the counter. "I'm fully authorized by the state of California to—"

But the woman didn't listen to him. She just walked back into a hallway on the far side of the office. Dan Rosenthal drummed his fingers on the counter for what seemed like a million years.

Finally this sort of hippie-looking guy with longish graying hair came out. "I'm Garland Shook," the man said, "headmaster of the Hartwell School. How about you come with me."

Rosenthal followed the man back into the office, but didn't sit in the chair. "Look, I just need to see a student of yours, Cody Jackson."

The man gave him a bland smile. "And might I ask why?"

"Sure," Dan Rosenthal said. "I'm about to place him under arrest."

ONE

RULE ONE:
BE YOURSELF

ONE WEEK EARLIER

Hey, so my name is Nathan McHugh.

I attend the Hartwell School outside Los Angeles. I'm recording this videotape for my summer video project for media arts class. My video is called—ta-da!—How To Get Elected President of the Junior Class.

Just in case you're wondering, yeah, I'm running for president of the class. I expect to win. No biggie. I've been president of our class for two years running.

Why do I get elected every time? Because I've figured out a strategy that works.

So here it is, guys: Ten simple rules for how

to get elected president of your high school class.

What I'm going to do is videotape everything I do as I run for president this year, show how the ten rules I've developed play out in the real world. Then you can see how it's done.

Oh, no, I'm gonna be late to school! Gotta roll.

Nathan was in a huge rush. The deadline to sign up for the student council elections was at the end of first period. His father had let him drive the Beemer for the first time and he had driven a little bit out of the way just to see what it was like to unwind the big V8 engine. Only . . . he'd gotten kind of turned around on the far side of Brentwood, and now he was not just late for school—he was in danger of missing the deadline to sign up for the class president race.

Class president! Hartwell's student council elections were always held on the last day of school before summer vacation. That was a week away. Now at the end of his sophomore year, Nathan had been class president two years running—but this election was the big one. Colleges really cared about your junior year. And if he was going to get into an Ivy, he needed every scrap of help he could get.

He was just a block from the school when he noticed the police car behind him, its blue lights flashing. He abruptly turned down the music on the stereo and pulled over, his heart pounding. *Oops!*

The door of the police car opened and a very tall, very muscular officer with skin the color of creosote climbed out. He walked up slowly, one hand on his gun, talking into the radio microphone on his shoulder. Finally he reached the window, bent down, and looked into the car.

"How you doing today, sir?" the officer said with exaggerated politeness.

"Uh, fine, Officer, sir," Nathan said.

The officer had on wraparound sunglasses so his eyes were hidden. "You know why I pulled you over?"

"Um . . ." Nathan swallowed. "I'm not sure."

The officer kept peering around the car like he was looking for something. He was chewing gum. "Nice car, sir."

"Thanks. It's my dad's."

"Mm-hm." The officer didn't exactly have his hand on his gun. But it was close. "You got a license?"

"Yes, sir."

"This car belong to you?"

Nathan shook his head. "I go to the Hartwell School. I was just driving to school."

"Mm-hm." The officer stood up, said some more things into his microphone, then leaned back down. "License and registration."

"Look, sir, I'm gonna be late to school if—"

The officer showed a bunch of very white teeth. "You could have some problems other than being late to school if you don't follow my instructions very carefully."

"Yes, sir. Can I take out my wallet?"

"Slowly, yes."

The officer looked at the license and registration for a very long time, then spoke into the microphone some more. Then the officer leaned over and said, "Nelson McHugh, that's your father?"

"Yes, sir." Nathan kept looking at the clock. Six minutes. He still had to park the car, get his stuff together, and get to class.

A change came over the officer's face. "*The* Nelson McHugh? You're his son?"

"Yes, sir."

"*The* District Attorney of Los Angeles County?"

"Yes, sir." Nathan's dad was in the newspapers pretty much every other day. People were always talking about how he might run for mayor or governor one of these days. Nathan didn't like making a big deal about it, though. A lot of kids at his school had well known parents. It was generally considered to be pretty uncool at Hartwell to blab about who your parents were.

Suddenly the officer smiled. "Well, son, you kind of shaved off a little bit of red light back there. But since your dad has done so much for the community . . ."

Nathan started to put the car in gear.

"Wait." Nathan's heart skipped a beat. But the officer was just reaching toward him with a business card with the LAPD logo on it. "Here you go, son. That's got my cell number on it. You ever need anything, you just call me."

Nathan put his signal on, merged slowly back into traffic, then floored it into the parking lot of the Hartwell School. If he missed the deadline he was going to—

Three minutes later he was inside the building, racing nervously down the hallway. He could see the piece of paper on the bulletin board in the hallway outside Dr. Shook's office. Somebody was standing in front of it—a girl with long, wavy hair.

He slowed to a halt, nearly out of breath. "Hi, Daley," he said. "What're you doing?"

"Signing up for the election," Daley Marin said. She was looking up and down the bulletin board. There were a bunch of pieces of paper, each one with a different office on it.

"Where's president?" she said.

"President?" Nathan said. "I thought you'd be running for secretary-treasurer."

"God, no!" Daley said. "Are you kidding me? Harvard won't even give you a second look unless you're at least president of your class."

"Well . . . last year you were . . ."

"Oh, there it is," she said. She took out a pen and started to write her name on the sign-up sheet for president of their class. The pen didn't work.

"Maybe you ought to sign up for a different office," Nathan said. "You know, I'm running for president, too."

"Oh, no, you should run for *vice* president," she said, shaking the pen.

"Hey, I'm applying to Harvard, too," he said. "Plus . . . I mean, it won't do you any good if you lose."

She looked at him sharply. "Lose? To *you?*"

Nathan shrugged, feeling a little irritated. "Well, *yeah*. I mean, I have been president of the class for the last two years."

"That's because I was secretary-treasurer of the student body last year," she said. It was like she wasn't even vaguely concerned about running against him. Was she serious?

Behind them someone cleared her throat. It was Mrs. Windsor, the school secretary. "Ten o'clock," she said. "Deadline's up."

Daley handed the sign-up sheet to Nathan. He signed his name, then handed it back to Mrs. Windsor. She collected the rest of the sign-up sheets, then disappeared.

"Don't come crying to me when you get rejected by Harvard," Nathan said.

"Nothing personal," Daley said. "But I'm gonna bury you."

Nathan laughed. Daley Marin. Right. Like she had a chance of beating him.

"You really ought to go for secretary-treasurer," Nathan said. "I mean, seriously, you're not exactly president material."

"Me?" Daley said scornfully. She shook her head like she was feeling sorry for him. "I was about to say the same thing about you. You've been president of the class for, what, two years? And what have you accomplished? Nothing. You're totally disorganized."

Nathan felt his face flush. Daley was very smart and organized, sure. But . . . *president?* People had to *like* you if you were going to be president. "You're not a people person, Daley. This is not your thing."

"You're always taking the easy road."

"You're not a natural leader."

"You're unfocused!"

"You're uptight!"

Daley and Nathan's faces had gotten closer and closer, and their voices had gotten louder and louder. Suddenly this was getting personal. Nathan wasn't about to let somebody this obnoxious and full of herself get in his way.

There was a brief pause and then they both spoke.

"You're toast!" Daley said.

"Dead meat!" Nathan said.

TWO

Eric McGorrill looked around to see if anybody in the computer center was watching. You weren't supposed to use the internet for anything but school work. *Yeah, right!* Like anybody paid attention to that rule.

The coast was clear, so he quickly logged in to this website—*www.highschooladvisor.com*—where you could get advice about tests and romance and college applications and stuff. He started typing:

Dear Advisor,

I'm totally crazy about this girl. I don't know why. I don't think I would even like her much if I knew her. But she's really beautiful and cool and I can't stop thinking about her. Also she's going out with this guy who's like really popular and friendly and plays football.

What should I do?

He stared at the message. Ugh! God! It was so pathetic and weak and stupid. He erased the message quickly.

Nah, he didn't need some dopey advisor to tell him what was up. He already knew what he needed.

Two things. First, he needed a chance to spend more time with her so she'd notice all his great personal qualities. Which was impossible at school. He didn't play sports or hang out with all the cool kids or do much of anything remarkable, so she wouldn't even talk to him. But in just about a week, that would change. They were going on this field trip for a week together.

And, second, he needed to get rid of the competition. By this time next week, she needed to not have a boyfriend anymore. Could he make that happen?

Eric smiled. Sure he could. That was just the kind of thing he was good at.

"Hey!" A loud voice brought Eric back to reality. "What are you smiling at, doofus?"

Someone smacked him in the back of the head and then a bunch of jocks started laughing. He turned and saw Rodney Alexander—this big guy that played center on the Hartwell School football team—standing behind him. Rodney Alexander drew back his hand like he was about to pop Eric again when one of the other guys grabbed his arm. It was Nathan McHugh, the second-string quarterback.

"C'mon, Rodney, cut him a break," Nathan said.

The jocks all walked away leaving Eric at the computer. Eric watched them go. Hey, maybe this was going to be even easier than he thought. *Bye-bye. Bye-bye, Mr. Popular-and-friendly-and-plays-on-the-football-team! Bye-bye!*

Melissa Wu sat with Nathan in an editing bay at the back of the media arts class. She'd just finished watching the brief video that Nathan had played.

"Wow!" she said. "Ten rules for how to get elected president of the class. That's gonna make a great summer project." It was only a little over a week until summer vacation. Every year they had to do a project over the vacation. This year Nathan's project was in media arts.

"I know!" Nathan said. "I was stressing all week about what to do for this project. And then this morning—boom!—it just came to me."

"So," Melissa said, "what *are* the ten rules?"

Nathan looked at her blankly. "Huh?"

"The ten rules for getting elected president."

"Oh . . ." Nathan cleared his throat. "Well. Actually, I . . . um . . . that's what I was hoping you could help me out with."

"What?" Melissa was puzzled. She didn't know anything about running for office.

"You know, help me brainstorm a little. I need to come up with the ten rules."

Melissa frowned. "Well, *you're* the one who's been president of our class for the past year."

"Two years, actually. But, see, the thing is—"

Before he could finish his sentence a loud female voice behind them shrieked, "Oh. My. God. Look at *you*, Melissa!"

Nathan and Melissa turned around. There was Nathan's girlfriend, Taylor Hagan. As usual, everything about her was perfect—her hair, her makeup, her nails, her shoes, her clothes. She was blond and beautiful and confident—totally unlike Melissa. Melissa always felt inadequate around Taylor.

"Your hair looks great, Melissa!" Taylor said. "That baby-doll pigtail thing is so *hot.*" She mussed Melissa's hair like she was some little kid, then plunked down in an editing chair and rolled the chair briskly between Nathan and Melissa. "Slide over, you have *got* to see this."

She hit the eject button, pulled out Nathan's disk, then slid her own DVD into the editing machine.

"We're kinda working here," Nathan said. "I'm trying to brainstorm about my summer project—"

"God, Nathan, stop being such a geek," Taylor said. "Why are you thinking about your summer project when school's not even over yet?" She hit the play button. "Anyway, check this out!"

Electronic dance music started blasting out of the speakers and then a picture of Taylor came on the screen. She was wearing a little gold dress that looked like it had cost about a zillion dollars.

She blew a kiss at the screen, turned so she was looking over her shoulder, eyelashes lowered. Then she sashayed toward the camera, her hips swiveling like a runway model.

"Remember that guy I told you about?" Taylor said.

"What guy?" Nathan said.

"You know, the one that works for Eddie da Costa, the designer?"

Melissa knew zero about fashion. But even she had heard of Eddie da Costa.

"Uh . . ." Nathan said, looking lost. Taylor punched him in the arm. "Ow!" Nathan said, laughing.

"Well, anyway, this guy, he's friends with Eddie da Costa and he does all their video shoots. And he thinks I could be a really big model."

"No kidding?" Nathan said.

"*Excuse* me, Melissa," Taylor said, squeezing her chair between Melissa and Nathan so that Melissa couldn't even see the screen. "Anyway, I got this guy to shoot some video of me! Hey! Maybe I could get him to do my summer project!"

"Wouldn't it be kind of cheating to have some professional video guy do your summer project?" Melissa said. "I mean, no offense, I'm not trying to . . ."

Melissa's voice trailed off. It was obvious Taylor wasn't listening to her anyway. "Here, here, here!" Taylor said. "Check this out, Nathan."

"Oh man!" Nathan said. "You look awesome. Who made that dress?"

"That's what I'm saying! That's an original da Costa!"

"Shut up!" Nathan said brightly. "A real da Costa? That is way too cool."

Melissa didn't like the way Nathan acted when he was around Taylor. It was like he was a whole different person.

"Hey, I got an idea," Melissa said. "Rule One. Be Yourself."

Nathan looked up from the video on the screen. "What?"

Taylor turned and glared at Melissa.

"Never mind." Melissa got the picture. Three was a crowd. She felt a brief stab of humiliation. Every time Taylor showed up, it was like Nathan totally forgot Melissa existed. "I'll just leave you little lovebirds."

Nathan pointed at her. "Hey, no, seriously, I heard you. Rule One for how to get elected president. Be Yourself. I love it. We'll finish brainstorming later, okay?"

"Sure," Melissa said, trying not to sound hurt.

Taylor turned back to the video. "Oh. My. God. This is awesome. Isn't this awesome?"

"It's awesome," Nathan said.

"It's *totally* awesome!" Taylor said.

"Totally," Melissa said. She stood there looking at the backs of their heads. Then she walked away.

THREE

"**S**ettle down! Settle down!" Dr. Shook held up his hands, trying to quiet everybody down. "Everybody sit down. I've got some good news and some bad news."

The camping club met after school in the Arts Center, a brand new building in the rear of the Hartwell School property. Eric slouched in his chair and looked around as the room filled. Taylor came in. Eric sat up straighter in his chair, stuck out his chest a little, leaned his head back slightly, trying his best to look cool. Then Nathan came in. Eric scowled. How did you compete with a guy like Nathan McHugh? Mr. Nice Guy. Mr. Football. Mr. Cute Dimples. All the girls at Hartwell got all googly-eyed every time he walked by.

The members of the camping club were

going to be leaving for their big eco-camping trip to Palau the day that summer vacation started. The only reason Eric was in the camping club was so he could be near Taylor. But the trip to Palau was going to totally rock. Palau was this little island paradise in the Pacific Ocean. They were going to fly there and hang out for ten days. Most of the kids were talking about how cool it was going to be to see all the monkeys and parrots and all this dumb crap. Eric just wanted to see Taylor in a bathing suit. After that, everything was gravy.

"Settle down!" Dr. Shook said again. "Guys, I've got some good news and some bad news. First the good news . . . we have an additional student joining us for the trip."

Dr. Shook gestured at the new guy sitting up near the front of the class. It was nearly impossible to get into Hartwell—but this guy had shown up suddenly right near the end of the year. Eric wondered who had pulled the strings to get this guy in.

"Most of you have met Cody Jackson. He just joined us last month. He's a scholarship student who is here with a special program called Operation Second Chance, sponsored by the mayor of Los Angeles. Cody, could you stand up?"

The new guy halfway got out of his seat, looking like he was bored by the whole business. "Actually, it's Jackson," he said. "Anybody calls me Cody, I'll bust 'em up."

The room was silent.

"Hey," the new kid said. "Joke." But he didn't

really look like he was joking. *Note to self,* Eric thought. *Don't get in this dude's way.*

Dr. Shook gave a sour smile, then said, "And now the bad news. Due to the fact that Cody— excuse me, *Jackson*—will be joining the trip, and because of recent increases in gas prices, I'm told that the charter plane we're taking from Guam to Palau is going to be significantly more expensive than anticipated. The result is that the club has a budget shortfall of twenty-three hundred dollars."

"What does that mean?" Daley said.

"It means that if you can't raise two thousand, three hundred dollars by next Thursday, there will be no eco-camping trip to Palau."

There was a long, dead silence.

"But . . . we've worked all year raising money!" Nathan said.

"This isn't fair!" Jory Twist said.

"I know, I know," Dr. Shook said. "But I have every confidence that a group of young people as creative and talented as you will come up with a way."

Taylor raised her hand. "Why don't Jackson's parents just pay for him to go?"

Dr. Shook looked uncomfortable. "Uh . . . well, no, that's actually not an option."

"Why not?" Taylor said.

"I'm sorry," Dr. Shook said. "It's just not. End of discussion. You're going to have to raise the funds as a group."

Great, Eric thought. *More freaking bake sales and car washes. More selling candles door-to-door.* Not that he'd actually *done* any of that himself. But still . . . it made him tired just thinking about it.

Nathan raised his hand. "The car wash we did back in the fall was pretty successful."

"Not twenty-three hundred dollars worth of successful," Daley said sharply.

"I think we picked the wrong location," Nathan said.

"You mean *you* picked the wrong location," Daley said.

"Whatever. The point is, if we do it over in Brentwood where I live, everybody drives high-end cars and they'll pay a mint to—"

"What about selling vegetarian sandwiches?" Abby Fujimoto said.

"Can I just say that's the most terrible idea I've ever heard in my life, Abby?" Eric said.

Abby looked at him like, *What?*

Kids started throwing out ideas for fund-raisers, each one dumber than the last. But finally everybody ran out of ideas.

"Anybody else?" Dr. Shook said. "Anybody?"

There was a brief silence.

"What about a contest?" Daley said.

"What kind of contest?" Dr. Shook said.

"Well, my stepmother's on the board of directors of the LA Zoo, and they just got this really cute, really rare monkey called a Palauan macaque. They haven't named it yet. What if we had a contest to name the monkey? It's perfect! A monkey from Palau. You buy a ticket and that gives you one chance to name the monkey. Then we'd have a big event at the end where there's a drawing, and whoever wins gets to name the monkey. Then we'd split the profits with the zoo. Everybody wins."

Eric rolled his eyes. *Name the monkey?* Trust a girl to come up with some kind of moronic idea like that. On the other hand, it wouldn't involve his doing any work. Definite plus. "Can I just say that's a really great idea," Eric said. "I mean, totally inspired."

"Thank you, Eric," Daley said.

"How much would we charge per ticket?" Nathan said.

"Five bucks, maybe? If just twenty percent of the kids at the school bought a ticket, that'd be a few thousand dollars. And some people might buy a bunch. At the end we'd have a big drawing and we could bring the monkey and . . ."

"That's *fun*," Dr. Shook said. "That is a really *fun* idea!"

Daley walked over to the computer and pulled up a picture of the monkey off the zoo's website. It had huge brown eyes and spiky fur that shot up off the top of its head in a comical way.

All the girls ran over and crowded around the screen. "It's so cute!" they were all saying. "It's so *cuuuuute!*"

The boys all looked at each other and shrugged.

"You know what?" Eric said. "If it means I don't have to sit around selling cookies in the parking lot of some strip mall, I'm totally for it."

"What kind of doofus would pay five bucks to name a monkey?" Nathan said.

"I would!" Melissa said.

"I would, too!" Abby said. "Oh, he's so sweet. Look at those eyes!"

"Nathan," Daley said, "you may recall that the last car wash we did raised about three hundred dollars."

"Four hundred and twenty," Nathan said. "Actually."

"Oh, terrific," Daley said. "That's only nineteen hundred dollars less than we need."

"Yeah, but I have the perfect location now."

"That's what you said last time, Nathan."

Dr. Shook held up his hands. "Okay, okay, guys. Tell you what. This name-the-monkey thing sounds great. But it's also rather ambitious. And we're very short on time. Daley, if you think you can put together such an event within the next two days, then go for it. If that doesn't work out, we'll have Nathan's car wash as a fallback plan. Deal?"

Daley and Nathan eyed each other for a minute, then nodded curtly. *What's eating them?* Eric wondered.

FOUR

At lunch, Nathan set his tray down across from Taylor. She was so busy flirting with Justin Meehan—a big, muscular guy who played tight end for the Hartwell Terriers— that she didn't notice him. At first that sort of thing had annoyed Nathan, but now he didn't take it seriously. That was just how Taylor was. If you wanted to go out with a girl like Taylor, you had to put up with some annoyances. Sometimes Nathan felt it had all been a big mistake—like, *How did I end up with the best-looking girl in the class?*

Taylor looked up. "Hi," she said, then sighed heavily.

"What's wrong?" Nathan said.

"Mr. Ellicott is such a *jerk*," she said, stabbing her fork into her salad. She was going through a vegetarian phase right now.

Mr. Ellicott was Taylor's chemistry teacher and a constant source of complaint. "He's a nice guy," Nathan said. "He's just tough."

"That's what I'm *saying*," she said. "He says he's going to give me a D. Me—a *D.*"

"Well, you have to admit chemistry's not exactly your best subject," Nathan said.

Taylor stared at him. "God! I can't believe you're taking his side."

"I'm just saying," Nathan said.

"Anyway, the point is, he's making me do this awful extra credit project." She reached across the table and said, "Come over and help me with it after school?"

"Hey, sure," Nathan said. "No problem."

"I thought you said you were running for president of the class," Justin said. "Don't you need to do posters and stuff?"

"Oh, man!" Nathan said. He hated disappointing Taylor. She always managed to make him feel bad. "I forgot, Taylor. I totally need to do all that election stuff."

Taylor blinked, looking at him pathetically. "You're not gonna help me?"

"Come on, Taylor, don't be like that." Since they had started going out, Nathan had been carrying her in three of her classes, practically doing all her homework for her. "Maybe I could—"

Taylor stood up sharply. "Forget it!" she said. "I'm only your girlfriend. I'm sure that's not a very important thing in your little world."

She walked away, swinging her hips. Feeling humiliated, he jumped up to follow after her—anxious to calm her anger—but he bumped the table, spilling his milk all over Art Nazel.

"Dude!" Art said.

"Sorry! Sorry!" Nathan was feeling more embarrassed and dopey by the moment.

By the time he'd gotten the milk mopped up, Taylor was gone. Sometimes Taylor was a little high maintenance. Maybe it was best to just let her cool off. He slumped back down in his chair.

"So I hear you're running against Daley Marin, girl of steel," Justin said.

"Girl of steel?"

"You got to admit, she's kinda tough."

Nathan made a dismissive face.

"You worried?"

"About Daley? Bro, are you kidding?"

Art and Justin looked at each other.

"What?" Nathan said. "You think I'm gonna lose to Daley?"

"Nah, nah," Art said. "It's just . . ."

"What?"

"Well, you know how she is," Justin said.

"Very competitive," Art said.

Nathan felt a sudden pang of nervousness. He'd never really thought about it that way. He'd just sort of figured everybody would vote for him because they'd always voted for him.

"Yeah," Nathan said. "But nobody really likes her, do they?"

"Oh, no," Art said. "Of course not. I'm just saying . . ."

"You'll definitely win, dude," Justin said. "Don't worry about that."

"Definitely," Art said.

"You're totally there," Lisa Reyes said. "All the cheerleaders are voting for you."

"Yeah," Art said. "You're a lock with the football team. Soccer will go for you, too."

"Thanks, guys," Nathan said. "That means a lot to me."

"Hey, don't *even* sweat it," Art said. "Daley Marin? Psshh. Please."

There was a brief silence.

"Of course, Daley plays clarinet," Art said. "She could get some votes from the band."

"Yeah. Science geeks, too."

"What about emos and goths, though?" Nathan said. The more he thought about it, the more nervous he got.

Art and Justin exchanged glances again. "Dude," Justin said. "You're overthinking this. You're in."

"Oh yeah," Art said. "Definitely."

Nathan stood up. "I better go find Taylor. She seemed a little peeved."

He put his tray on the conveyor belt at the front of the room, then walked out into the hallway. For some reason he was feeling unsettled. Surely he couldn't lose to Daley. Could he?

He saw Daley across the hallway having an intense conversation with some girls from the band.

They were all nodding their heads at her like she was saying something really brilliant.

Hmm.

Nathan didn't see Taylor anywhere in the hallway. Why did she always get bent out of shape when Nathan didn't do exactly what she wanted?

He was looking around when he noticed the new guy, Jackson, standing by the door, looking out at the quad.

"Did you happen to see Taylor go by here? Blond girl? Beautiful? Long hair?"

The new guy shook his head. "Sorry."

Nathan stepped forward, held out his hand. Never hurt to be friendly. Plus, maybe he could pick up a vote while he was at it. "I'm Nathan. I haven't introduced myself. I'm in the camping club, too. It's Jackson, right?"

"Jackson, yeah." Jackson shook his hand.

"So, what school did you go to before this?"

"Caesar Chavez High School."

"Chavez!" Nathan's eyebrows went up. Chavez was in a seriously bad neighborhood. Not many kids from that part of LA went to Hartwell.

Jackson shrugged.

"So how'd you end up here?"

"Applied. Got in."

Nathan waited for Jackson to expand on that. But he didn't. Nathan couldn't put his finger on what it was, but for some reason he was curious about the guy.

"So you live over near Chavez then, huh?"

Jackson shook his head no.

Nathan was puzzled. If he didn't live near Chavez, how come he'd gone to school there? "I've seen you out there at the bus stop after school," Nathan said. "Must take you a while to get back over there."

"I moved."

"Oh, yeah? Where?"

Jackson looked out the window. "Couple miles that way."

The bell rang for sixth period to begin. Riding the bus—man, that would be a drag! Nathan figured he ought to help the guy out a little. Plus, it would give him a chance to get to know the guy a little better. "I got my dad's car today. You want a ride?"

"Sure."

"Meet you outside after school," Nathan said.

Jackson nodded, but didn't say anything else. No "thank you," no "nice to meet you," no nothing. *Weird*, Nathan thought.

As he turned around, a perky-looking girl from the ninth grade was standing there with a clipboard. She wore a button that said DALEY FOR PRESIDENT.

"Hi!" she said. "We're doing a survey for Daley Marin's campaign. Would you like to participate?"

Nathan blinked. "A *survey*?" Man. Daley was really taking this thing way too seriously. Nathan was starting to get a bad feeling about this election. He was gonna have to get busy. He felt his stomach start to knot up. *What a day.*

FIVE

RULE TWO:
IT PAYS TO ADVERTISE

By the end of school, Daley was full of confidence and enthusiasm. Nathan was a nice guy, but she shouldn't have a problem beating him. He was too disorganized. Her survey was all finished. Her little stepbrother, Lex, who was a computer whiz, had come up with a program to tally the results, and a freshman girl was pecking all the data into a computer in the Science Center. Daley watched over her shoulder for a minute to make sure she wasn't messing it up, then took out her cell phone and called her stepmother.

"Gwen, hi!" she said. "I have a great idea."

"Hi, honey," her stepmother said. "What's your idea?"

Daley's mother had died about five years ago, and her father had remarried pretty soon after that. At first Daley had felt betrayed. But her stepmother was a pretty cool person and now she was really close to her.

"Well," Daley said, "the camping club needs to raise two thousand, three hundred dollars for our trip to Palau. Somebody screwed up the budget, I guess. So anyway, I had this idea that we could do a contest to name the new monkey at the zoo."

Brief pause. "What monkey?" her stepmom said. Daley could tell she was dubious.

"The one with the spiky hair, the Palauan macaque? Remember you were telling me—"

"Oh, right."

"And remember how you were saying that the zoo lets big donors name animals?"

"Okay . . ."

"Well, what if we just let the winner of a drawing pick the name? We'd sell tickets at school for a week and then have this big event to cap the whole thing. We'd bring out that guy, Ranger Bob or whatever his name is?—the guy that does the animal outreach program?"

"Ranger Mike."

"Ranger Mike. Right. We bring out Ranger Mike and he'd bring the monkey and do a little program about monkeys or whatever. All the Hartwell parents could come. Plus people from the general public who like animals. We'd sell more tickets at the event. Then at the end we draw the winning ticket and name the monkey. We split the money with the zoo. The first twenty-three hundred dollars goes to the camping club, and everything else goes to the zoo. Isn't that a *great* idea?"

Daley's stepmother cleared her throat. "Well. Um. It sounds admirable. When were you thinking of having this big event?"

"Next Thursday. The last day of school."

"Next *Thursday*! Wow, that's kind of short notice."

"Come on, Gwen, what's there to lose? Besides, it's be free publicity for the zoo."

Daley's stepmother didn't say anything for a minute.

"Just call up the director of the zoo," Daley said. "Please! Ask her. What's the worst that could happen? She says no, right?"

There was a long pause. "I'll call you back," Daley's stepmother said.

Daley hung up the phone, pumped her fist in the air. "Yes!"

A couple more kids had filtered into the Science Center. "You guys here to help with the campaign?"

Their heads nodded.

"Okay, good. Jory, could you get them started working on folding fliers? I need to run down and talk to Dr. Shook."

Jory Twist was an underclass girl who was always following Daley around looking all worshipful. Daley had figured she might as well put her to work.

"Oh, I forgot," Daley said as she paused at the door. "The website. Anybody here know how to design websites?"

A skinny boy with glasses held up a finger tentatively.

"Excellent. What's your name again?"

"Ian. Ian Milbauer."

"Great. Walk with me, Ian. I have some ideas."

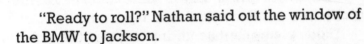

"Ready to roll?" Nathan said out the window of the BMW to Jackson.

"S'up," Jackson said, raising his chin slightly. Instead of getting in the car, he just stood there, looking at it.

"Hop in," Nathan said.

Jackson finally slid into the back seat. "Nice," he said. "I've only seen these in magazines."

"My regular car's just a Nissan," Nathan said. "It's in the shop, so Dad loaned me his."

Jackson shook his head like he couldn't believe anybody would trust a kid with a car like this. It didn't seem like such a big deal to Nathan. There were kids at Hartwell who had cars of their own as nice as this one. "This thing must fly, huh?" Jackson said.

Nathan laughed. "Probably. But Dad would kill me if he found out I was driving it fast."

Jackson gave him a look like he was a total sissy. Nathan turned on the stereo. All it had in the CD player was his dad's music. It started playing some ancient Smokey Robinson song.

"Sorry," Nathan said. "My old man's tunes."

He started driving. Jackson took a CD out of his book bag and slid it into the stereo.

After a few seconds, some very hardcore rap started coming out of the speakers. Jackson turned it up. Loud. They pulled up at light. A middle-aged white woman with frosted hair looked over at them, then reached over to hit her door-lock button. Nathan smiled pleasantly at her. She avoided his gaze, then roared off when the light turned green.

"You gonna let some old lady take you?" Jackson said.

"Hey, I'm just trying to get home," Nathan said. "I'm not like Joe Streetracer."

"I noticed," Jackson said. Then he turned up the music some more.

Nathan listened to the music for a minute. It was weird. He could understand about a tenth of what the rapper guy was saying.

"What is this?" Nathan said when the song was over.

"Samoan rap."

"Samoan as in . . . guys from the Polynesian island of Samoa?"

Jackson nodded. "Lot of Samoans at Chavez."

"Really. You must have been, like, the only white guy."

"Pretty much."

"How was that?"

"How do you think?" Jackson said.

"Hey, sorry," Nathan said. "I'm not trying to ask a lot of personal questions or anything."

"Good," Jackson said.

Whoa. Conversation stopper!

Nathan braked at another light. Jackson looked over at the car next to them, a red Porsche convertible. A chubby bald guy sat in the driver's seat, an expression on his face like he was real impressed with himself. Jackson reached over in front of Nathan and honked the horn.

The bald guy looked over at them like, *What?*

"Why'd you do that?" Nathan said to Jackson.

Jackson turned toward the guy in the Porsche and said, "My friend here thinks Porsches are for girls."

"Yeah?" the bald guy said.

Jackson looked over at Nathan and gave him an innocent look.

"Oh, come on," Nathan said.

Jackson didn't move a muscle. Nathan could feel his heart racing. This was so *stupid*. He snuck a glance at the chubby guy. He was giving Nathan a stare, like, *Bring it on, son.* Nathan instinctively disliked the guy. And now the guy was going to beat his pants off.

Nathan took a deep breath. The light turned green. Without really planning to, Nathan stomped on the gas. The BMW jumped forward. Nathan had never realized just how powerful the car was. His dad always drove it very slowly and carefully. But now the thing was pinning him to the seat. The Porsche leapt off the line with a howl of tires behind them.

Nathan had a jump on the Porsche, though, and was leading by about half a car length. His heart was pounding and his hands were all sweaty. Cars parked along the side of the street whizzed by. Ahead of them, the street was clear for a pretty long way. Nathan halfway hoped somebody would pull out, giving him an excuse to slow down. No such luck.

The Porsche was starting to gain on him. He looked down at the speedometer. He was going a hundred and five. *A hundred and five! What am I thinking?*

He immediately let off the gas and the Porsche pulled up and passed him.

The bald guy waved over his shoulder and yelled something.

Jackson shook his head sadly.

Now Nathan felt like a loser. He hesitated for a moment, them stomped the gas again. The big BMW started accelerating again. 105. 110. 115.

The Porsche started losing ground.

120. 125.

They blew by the Porsche. At the next light, the Porsche abruptly slowed, put on its signal, turned, disappeared.

Nathan let off the gas. His heart was slamming in his chest and his hands were trembling. "Okay, I think that was about the stupidest thing I've ever done," he said.

"Nice," Jackson said softly. "*Very* nice."

He let off the gas until the car was down to 65.

It was still pretty fast, but after the speed he'd been going, it felt like he was crawling.

"Uh . . ." Jackson said, pointing a finger in front of them. "You might wanna—"

He didn't finish his sentence. Nathan looked up and an ancient pickup truck had pulled out in front of them. There was nowhere to go. Nathan slammed on his brakes. But it was obvious they weren't going to stop in time.

He cut the wheel. There was a loud bang as they jumped the curb and for a moment they seemed to be floating in the air. Next thing Nathan knew, there was a crunch and they came to rest. In a ditch.

"Oh man! My dad's gonna kill me!"

Nathan jumped out of the car, ran around it, looking to see if there was any damage. He couldn't see any. He hopped back in and attempted to back up. The wheels spun, but the car wouldn't move.

Nathan tried to think. *Okay, okay. What should I do? Call Dad?* No, that was totally the last resort. This was bad. This was terrible. He was *so* busted.

Then something struck him. Wait a minute! He pulled out the card that the policeman had given him that morning, dialed the number.

"Uh, hi, Officer," Nathan said. "This is Nathan McHugh. You pulled me over this morning outside the Hartwell School? Yeah, I'm fine, thanks. But I have a little problem . . ."

After Nathan finished his call, Jackson said, "Who was that?"

"Oh, this police officer I know."

Jackson blinked, then opened his door and got out of the car. Nathan was puzzled.

"Where you going, man?"

"Home."

"The policeman said he'd have tow truck here in about ten minutes."

"I'm going anyway."

"Why?"

"Trust me," Jackson said. "You don't want me around when LAPD shows up."

"What do you mean?"

But Jackson didn't answer. He just walked away. *Okay,* Nathan thought. *Scary!*

When Jackson got back to the house where he was living, his foster mother was waiting at the door. Her name was Elaine Berkhalter. She was a nice enough lady, but kind of strict.

"You're late," she said. "You were supposed to meet with your caseworker from the Department of Social Services. Remember? Mr. Rosenthal?"

"This guy from school gave me a ride," he said. "But then he wrecked his car."

Her eyes narrowed for a moment. "Are you all right?" she said finally.

"I'm fine. He just ran off the road. Nothing serious."

"What was his name?"

He frowned. "Why?"

"I'd just like to call to make sure he's okay, too."

Jackson looked at her for a moment. It was obvious she was calling to check up on him. Jackson felt a burst of anger. "Nathan McHugh."

"Isn't that the name of the District Attorney of LA County?"

"No, you're thinking of Nelson McHugh. I think he's Nathan's dad."

"My goodness," she said. "Aren't *we* hanging out with the highfalutin' types."

Jackson walked into the house and a balding man with a wincing smile stood up from the couch. Jackson remembered him from an earlier meeting. He had seemed like a jerk. The second he saw him, he felt all knotted up in his stomach. He couldn't stand having people telling him what to do. Especially self-important creeps like this Rosenthal guy, who just seemed to enjoy making life hard on other people.

"Hi, Cody," Mr. Rosenthal said.

"I go by Jackson." He had told this to the guy at least five times. It was obvious by now that the guy was just jerking him around.

"Mm-hm," the man said with a bland smile that showed he didn't care one way or the other. "You want to sit?"

Jackson sat.

There was a long silence. The caseworker studied Jackson for a while. "So," he said finally.

"What's it been, a month or so that you've been at Hartwell?"

Jackson nodded.

"I forgot, man of few words," Mr. Rosenthal said. "Look, reason I swung by, I just found out about this supposed trip you're taking."

"I told you about it before," Jackson said. "Twice."

"Yeah. Well. Little problem, Cody. Strictly speaking, you're on probation for that little episode last year that you and your buddies were involved in."

"I wasn't involved. I was just there."

"Whatever. Bottom line, you need written permission to go on this little trip to . . ."

"Palau."

"Palau, right, Palau. Anyway, I just don't want you getting your hopes up. I'm doing the paperwork, but it may not be possible."

Jackson examined the man's face. Which led him to believe the guy was not being all that truthful. The guy was probably doing everything he could to keep Jackson from getting permission to go. Most likely all he had to do was fill out some form and it was done. But it had been obvious since their first meeting that—for some reason— this guy had it in for Jackson.

Jackson was doing fine in school and hadn't had any disciplinary problems. This was some kind of power play on Mr. Rosenthal's part. Jackson looked at his watch. Just being near this guy for two minutes made him feel all squirmy, like someone had locked him in a cage.

"Got someplace important to be?" Mr. Rosenthal said.

Jackson shrugged. In fact, he did have someplace he needed to be. But he wasn't in the mood to explain.

Suddenly Mr. Rosenthal stood up. "All right, then. In spite of your sullen attitude, I'm gonna go to bat for you about this trip." He eyeballed Jackson for a minute. "But you better keep your nose clean."

The caseworker left without saying another word.

Jackson stood up and walked back to his bedroom.

"There's ice cream in the freezer," his foster mother called to him. "Rocky Road!"

Rocky Road. Jackson wasn't big on ice cream with all that lumpy junk in it. What was wrong with plain old chocolate or vanilla? "No, thanks," he said.

Then he went back to his room. Elaine Berkhalter had two other foster kids—both of them going to public school—and Jackson had to share his room with both of them. There was hardly room to breathe. Davion and Tre were already in the room, playing with their Power Rangers. They were a lot younger than Jackson. It got on his nerves having them in his room. Until he got taken away from her, it had always been just him and his mom. And half the time his mom hadn't been at home, anyway. He had a hard time getting used to having other kids crawling all over.

"Jackson! Jackson!" Davion and Tre yelled. "Play with us!"

"Hey, guys. What's up?"

"Play Power Rangers! Play Power Rangers!"

"Sorry, y'all. I gotta go study."

He reached underneath his bed and came out with a long piece of metal with a sharp point on the end.

"What's that?" Tre said.

"Yeah! What's that?"

"Nothing." He slid the steel into his book, then went back out into the living room. Elaine was watching some preacher on TV.

"I'm going out," he said.

"Where are you going?"

"To the library. I need to study."

"Why can't you study here?"

"I can't work with Tre and Davion playing Power Rangers."

"I'll make sure they—"

"Nah, nah, let them have fun. I can concentrate better at the library."

"I'll give you a ride."

He shook his head. "I like to walk."

"But it's a long way. It's—"

He walked out the front door, letting the screen bang behind him.

The neighborhood was typical for this part of the city. Little bungalows with steel bars over the doors, an occasional runty palm tree in the yard. It wasn't a terrible neighborhood. But he was pretty sure it wasn't like the ones his classmates at the Hartwell School were living in.

As he walked, he felt like he could finally breathe again. Nothing against Elaine Berkhalter—she was doing what she could—but it just wasn't home. He felt claustrophobic all the time. The TV blasting, the other kids running around and yelling, Elaine hovering all the time, asking him where he was going, where he'd been, what he was doing.

Out here, walking down the street, he felt free. He walked toward the library. But when he reached Easton Street, instead of turning left, he turned right. Eventually he got to Pulliam Street, where there was a strip mall full of businesses with all the signs written in Vietnamese. A bright yellow Honda with nice rims and extra wide tires sat at one corner of the lot, Samoan rap blasting out the door. As he approached the car, the man in the driver's seat turned toward him. It was Big Jay. He had a big, black Samoan tribal tattoo running down the side of his face.

"You're late," Big Jay said.

"Hey, some things happened."

Big Jay cocked his head toward the back door. "Get in, bro. You got work to do."

Jackson got in and the Samoan music rolled over him. He blew out a long breath. Okay. Now he was feeling better. Like a five hundred pound weight had been taken off his shoulders.

Daley walked into Dr. Shook's office feeling excited.

"So it's all set, Dr. Shook!" she said. "The zoo is willing to do it. Ranger Mike's coming out with the monkey."

Dr. Shook looked up from his desk and smiled. "Great."

"I was wondering, though—we have a student assembly coming up soon. Do you think one of us could have about two minutes at the beginning to announce the contest?"

"Sure, we could fit you in."

"Great. I'll see if we can get the monkey out here."

Dr. Shook frowned. "You want to bring the monkey to the assembly?"

"Why not?"

"I'm not sure if that's wise."

"Dr. Shook, please! You have to see how cute it is! The kids'll go nuts, and then they'll buy more tickets."

Dr. Shook looked thoughtful. "Somebody would be here from the zoo to take care of it?"

"Of course."

"Well, what the heck." Dr. Shook smiled broadly. He leaned back in his chair and laced his fingers across his chest. "I am more impressed by you every day."

"Thank you, Dr. Shook."

"You'll be applying early decision to Harvard, won't you?"

"Yes, sir."

"Have I written your recommendation for the application yet?"

"Not yet, sir. I won't be applying for another year."

"Well, you be sure to let me know whenever you need it." Dr. Shook beamed at her.

"I appreciate it."

S I X

The doorbell rang and Nathan opened the door. He was hoping it would be Taylor. After their little spat at lunch, he'd wanted to make up. But it wasn't Taylor. It was just Melissa.

"Oh, hi," Nathan said.

Melissa frowned. "You look disappointed."

"Oh, no, it's not that. I've just been leaving messages with Taylor all afternoon and she won't call me back."

Melissa didn't say anything. But she looked like she wanted to.

"What?" Nathan said.

"Nothing." Melissa hesitated. Nathan knew that Melissa had never liked Taylor. Melissa was his best friend—always had been. But there'd never been anything romantic between them. "So, who else is coming to help out with the election?"

"Art, Justin, Lisa—a few others said they'd come."

"Cool. What do we need to do?"

"I guess we'll do some posters." Nathan's cell phone rang. "Hold on," he said.

It was Justin. "Dude, I know I promised to come over and help out," Justin said. "But I totally forgot I had that test in math."

"Hey, no problem," Nathan said. "I've got plenty more people coming."

He hung up and then said, "Art said he'd bring poster board, so I guess we have to wait till he gets here."

They went into the kitchen and Nathan's mother, a tall, mocha-skinned woman with lots of silver bracelets, gave Melissa a big hug. "You want some cake, Mel?" she said. "It's chocolate."

"That'd be great, thanks."

Nathan's mother nudged Mel. "I can't get his little girlfriend to eat anything but salad," she said. "I don't trust a girl who doesn't like chocolate."

"Mom!" Nathan said. He was tired of hearing her rag on Taylor all the time.

Melissa helped herself to a glass of milk and started eating the cake.

The phone rang. It was Art. "I feel like a jerk, but Dad wants me to clean the pool tonight." There was a brief pause. "I could, uh, get that poster board stuff. If you want."

"Nah, nah, that'd be silly."

"Sorry."

"Yeah, no, hey, it's not a problem." Nathan was starting to feel like everybody was jumping ship on him. What was the deal? Didn't they even care if he got elected?

He hung up the phone. Nathan frowned. "Well, looks like Art's blowing us off, too."

"You want me to run out to Target and get the stuff?" Melissa said, her mouth full of chocolate cake. "Mmm! Mrs. McHugh, this is the greatest."

"Made from scratch."

Nathan sighed. For some reason he was suddenly feeling nervous.

Eventually Melissa went out for the poster board, returning around quarter to eight. No one had shown up to help. Not Lisa, not Jeff, not Kristin. Nathan was feeling deflated.

Melissa must have seen the disappointed look on Nathan's face because the first thing she said was, "Hey! It'll be *fine*. You and me can get everything done."

They got the poster board out, and some Magic Markers.

"So," Melissa said. "What's your slogan? What's your campaign theme?"

"Slogan?" Nathan blinked. "I was kinda just thinking, like, Nathan for President."

Melissa looked at him for a long time. "Okay ..." she said. "That'll work."

She slowly lettered her first sign in red ink.

NATHAN McHUGH FOR PRESIDENT!

Then she held it up. "What do you think?"

Nathan smacked himself in the forehead. "Okay, that does kinda suck, doesn't it?" What had he been *thinking*? He had taken this whole thing for granted.

"We need something a little more . . ."

"Catchy."

"Punchy. Yeah."

Nathan heard the garage door motor kick on. That meant his dad was arriving home from work. Nathan felt an anxious twitch in his gut. He was praying his dad wouldn't be able to figure out that he'd run the Beemer into the ditch that afternoon. After a minute the door from the garage opened with a loud, sharp bang. Not good.

"Uh-oh," Nathan said.

"So," Lex said to Daley, "did you do the survey?"

"Uh-huh," Daley said. She handed him a printout of the responses her girls had gotten. The survey had been Lex's idea. He liked anything that involved numbers.

"This is very interesting," Lex said.

"Look, I've got to call the printer about my signage and then get busy with my homework," she said.

"Signage?" Lex said. "What's that?"

"That's advertising lingo for signs."

"Oh. You mean posters?"

Lex was a very nice kid, but he was good at getting under your skin. She had too much work to do to sit around blabbing with him. "Look, I appreciate your helping me with the poll. But I have to get this math done."

Lex shrugged and walked away.

Daley sat down at the kitchen table and started doing her homework. She was feeling a little panicky. All of her work on the campaign had set her back on her homework. And she had final exams coming up next week.

She'd been working for about an hour when her father got home. He was kind of a workaholic and rarely got home until after supper. He was a tall, friendly-looking man with sandy hair and thick glasses. "Hi, Daley," he said. "How was the day?"

"Busy," she said.

"I'll bet!" he said. "Gwen told me about this name-the-monkey thing you're planning. How's that going?"

"Great," she said. "I was hoping you'd have some ideas on how to promote the event."

"I'll give it some thought," he said. "Oh, hey, and while we're on the subject of promotion, I got your posters back from the printer." He left the room.

While she was waiting for her father to come back with the posters, Lex came down the stairs from his room. "Okay," he said. "I think you'll find my analysis to be very interesting."

"Your *analysis*?" Lex didn't talk like a normal ten-year-old. But then, he wasn't really a normal ten-year-old. He was one of these boy genius types. Still, he was only ten. It didn't seem like he'd have anything useful to say about her campaign.

"Sit down," he said, "and let me go over the numbers."

She sighed loudly. If she didn't humor him, he'd be bugging her all night. "Okay, okay, okay." She sat on the couch.

He spread the sheets out in front of her on the table. "Okay," he said, "first I want you to tell me who you think is going to vote for you."

She squinted at him. "What do you mean?"

"Jocks? Cheerleaders? The band kids? Nerds? Freaks? Goths?"

"Oh. Well, look, here's the thing. Nathan is a very nice guy. Everybody likes Nathan. And deservedly so. But he's just not presidential timber."

"Presidential timber." He looked at her blankly.

"People will recognize that I'm more focused than him. So they'll vote for me."

Lex looked at her for a minute, like he was waiting for the smart part of what she had to say. Finally he said, "That's it? That's your strategy?"

She shrugged. "Well . . . yeah."

He shook his head dismissively. "Nah. That's no good." He pushed the paper in front of her. "See, basically you can categorize everybody at your school. Boys, girls, jocks, geeks, band people, whatever. And each of these groups has issues that interest them. I asked questions here that pretty much show which group the person is fitting into. So that allows me to categorize everybody. Then I asked people to name the things they most wanted changed about the school." Lex looked up at her. "Your dad told me all about this. This is what he does at the advertising agency. Is any of this ringing a bell?"

"Hey, I just gave your questions to those girls."

"So you didn't even look at them."

Daley rolled her eyes.

"Okay, humor me. If you had to guess, will the jocks vote for you?"

Daley shook her head no.

"Cheerleaders?"

"No."

"Geeks?"

"Yes."

"Band girls?"

"Look, what's your point?"

Lex looked at her with unblinking eyes. "Every jock in the poll said they want more towels in the gym locker room."

Daley felt a flash of irritation. "More *towels*? That's idiotic."

"*You* think so. But you're not out there in the gym taking a shower twice a day. To them, hey, they'd rather have more towels than an entire new wing on the science building."

Daley shook her head. "That's just dumb."

"Here's the point. Promise more towels in the locker room? You'll get half the jocks. Even if they like Nathan more than you. Same with the freaks. Same with the goths and any other little clique or group you can think of. There's an issue for every single group in the school. And it's all right here on this paper. Every time people run for office in school, they're like, *I'm more qualified, I'm a nice guy, I have beaucoup school spirit . . .*" Lex made a farting noise. "Nice guy? School spirit? Who gives a crap? The jocks want more towels."

Daley's eyes started to widen. Once again, she'd underestimated her little brother.

"It's all right there." Lex rapped on the printout with his knuckles. "The Daley Marin twelve-point program to improve the Hartwell School."

She stared at the printout. Daley did not like admitting that other people were right. But by gosh, Lex was totally right. "Lex . . . you are a genius!"

"Sure." Lex had a pleased smile on his face. "Tell me something I don't know."

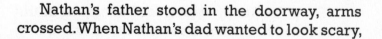

Nathan's father stood in the doorway, arms crossed. When Nathan's dad wanted to look scary, he did a pretty good job. He didn't say anything, just stood there looking at Nathan.

Oh no. Nathan felt his stomach twist again. "Uh... I was gonna tell you, Dad!"

"Were you?"

"Maybe I better go," Melissa said.

A smile broke out on Nathan's father's face as he turned toward her. "Hi, Melissa. Great to see you. Don't count on having Nathan pick you up in the morning, huh?"

"Nice to see you, too," Melissa said. "Bye!" Then she was gone.

"Look, Dad, the situation was just that this guy in this huge old truck pulled out in front of me and I kind of had to drive off the road to avoid him."

The smile that Nathan's father had given Melissa was very much gone. "Hence all the grass and dirt stuck underneath my car."

"Um—"

"And the part you're skipping is . . ."

Nathan tried his best to look innocent. He sure didn't *feel* innocent, though.

"The police commissioner called me personally, son. Said one of his officers had to call an LAPD tow truck for you? Pulled you out of a ditch? Y'all shared a little joke about possibly being involved in a street race just prior to the accident? Hm?"

"Uh . . ." Nathan swallowed. How in the world had the police commissioner of the entire city of

Los Angeles found out about some little thing like this? This was disastrous!

"See, son, you didn't lie to me just now." His father's face was impassive. "But you didn't tell me the whole truth."

"Yes, sir," Nathan said. "I was going to, but—"

"Uh-huh. Uh-huh. Think about that while you do without your allowance this month."

"A month!"

"Do I need to go into one of my usual long and boring stories about all the jobs I worked at night so I could afford to go to college? How I had to study while I was on break, carry hundred pound bags of cement on the loading dock at the—"

"No, Dad. I have all those stories memorized, I promise."

"Good. Because sometimes you don't act like it. Sometimes you don't seem to appreciate all that you've been given."

Nathan hated this. His dad was master of the guilt trip. Nathan hung his head. "I know."

Nathan's father looked down at the campaign poster on the floor. "Huh," he said, frowning thoughtfully. "Don't you need a slogan or something? Little bit of excitement? Little pizzazz? I mean . . . *Nathan for President*? No offense, that seems a little uninspiring."

Gee, Dad, thanks for making me feel better.

SEVEN

Nathan had agreed to meet Melissa an hour before first period so they could put up posters. But he got a little behind and showed up ten minutes late. Melissa was waiting for him by the main entrance to the school. She looked apprehensive.

"Daley got here about half an hour ago," she said. "With, like, eight other people. She had kind of a huge stack of posters."

They walked into the front door of the main classroom building. There were about ten posters hanging on the walls already. Huge posters. Professionally printed.

VOTE DALEY
SHE'S GONNA FIX IT!

In the center of the poster was a picture of Daley, a sort of glamour shot that made her look beautiful and intelligent and sincere all at the same time. The posters even had a little logo down in the corner.

Nathan couldn't believe it. Totally professional. "Oh *man!*" he said.

He looked at the amateurish posters that Melissa was carrying—NATHAN FOR PRESIDENT, hand-lettered in Magic Marker—and suddenly felt unprepared and embarrassed.

"She's got a *website*?" Melissa said.

"Where?"

Melissa pointed. At the bottom of every poster, there it was: *www.daleyrocks.com.*

They walked glumly down the hallway. There were printed sheets of paper stuck on every locker, each one with a question on it. *Tired of running out of towels? Daley's gonna fix it. (See daleyrocks.com for details.)*

Gamers. Feel like second-class citizens? Daley's gonna fix it.

Why is the art department always out of paint? Daley's gonna fix it.

"Tired of running out of *towels*?" Melissa said. "Boy, she's really picking the important issues, huh?"

Nathan looked at her sharply. "Mel, it's a serious problem. We never have any towels in the locker room after games. Somebody needs to do something about it."

"Maybe you should vote for Daley," Melissa said dryly.

Nathan's shoulders sagged. "This stinks."

"What are you gonna do about it?"

Nathan took all of his junky posters out of her hands, walked down to the trash can at the end of the hall, and dumped them. The loud clang reverberated up and down the empty hallway.

"We spent three hours working on those!" Melissa said.

"They're not good enough," Nathan said. "Look, I underestimated the competition here. I've never been up against anybody who was quite as prepared as Daley. In my other elections, everybody just kind of slapped up a few crummy posters and that was it. We have to do better."

"Okay."

"Fresh ideas. Clean sheet of paper. Hard-hitting new program. Serious ad campaign. We're taking the gloves off." He was trying to sound confident. But he didn't feel that way.

From the far end of the hallway Nathan heard some noise. Then a gaggle of young girls appeared, Daley in the middle of them, talking rapidly. They all looked busy and enthusiastic.

Daley stopped in front of them. "Hi, Nathan. Hi, Melissa. Putting up posters?"

"No," Nathan said. "Mine aren't, uh, back from the printer yet." He tried to position himself in front of the trash can so she wouldn't see the junky posters he had just thrown away.

"Cool," Daley said. "Hey, glad I caught you.

I'm trying to set up this whole name-the-monkey thing. Could I get you to help with publicity?"

"Well . . ."

"Oh, come on. You're not still bent out of shape about the car wash thing, are you?"

"Nah, nah!" Nathan smiled. He wondered if it looked as fake and anxious as it felt.

"Okay, good. This is gonna be the event of the year. I know we'll make loads of money for our trip *and* for the zoo. I'll e-mail you with my ideas." She smiled brightly, and she and her entourage hustled off down the hallway.

"Bye," Nathan said glumly.

After Daley was gone, Melissa said, "Does she scare you a little bit?"

"No!" Nathan swallowed. "I'm still gonna kick her butt."

"So. Fresh ideas. Clean sheet of paper. Hard-hitting new program. What do you have in mind, Nathan?"

Nathan looked around blankly. Everywhere his eyes came to rest, there was a poster saying how Daley was going to fix it. He felt like he was being squashed from all directions.

"I have no idea."

EIGHT

RULE THREE:
FIND AN ISSUE THAT
EVERYBODY IN THE SCHOOL
CAN GET BEHIND

"I know! I know!" Nathan said excitedly. "A new gym."

"A what?" Melissa said.

It was the next morning, and she and Nathan had been trying to think up a good issue for the campaign since they'd seen Daley's posters the previous day.

"Listen, Mel," he said, "I came up with Rule Three last night. *Find an issue everybody in your class can get behind.* See? Everybody knows the gym is the most decrepit building on campus. Right? So we just need a new one. It's a winner."

Melissa felt a little confused. A new gym. It wasn't like the student council could build a whole gym. "Yeah, but . . . do you think it's even vaguely possible to do that?"

Nathan shrugged. "Hey, I don't know. But

nobody thought we could go to the moon until that president announced that we were going to do it. See? A big goal, a big challenge! It's perfect. It'll show I've got vision. I'm a Big Idea guy."

"Yeah, but—"

A couple of kids walked by and Nathan said, "Hey guys, what's up? Everybody voting for me? Excellent! Here, have a button. Have a button!" He handed each boy a NATHAN FOR PREZ button that he and Melissa had made at lunch.

"Wouldn't that be really expensive?" Melissa said. "I'm not trying to be critical, but, like, who would pay for it?"

Nathan shrugged. "Who cares? The main thing is, we need to get posters up saying what I'm going to do."

Suddenly an idea struck Melissa. "You know the large format printer in the media arts classroom? The one you taught me to use?"

"Brilliant! Could you take a minute to buzz off a few dozen posters after school?"

"Uh . . . sure." As soon as she said it, though, Melissa realized that it would take about three hours just to print up a few posters. She'd barely have time to do her homework tonight.

"Great! Man, this is such a brilliant idea."

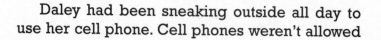

Daley had been sneaking outside all day to use her cell phone. Cell phones weren't allowed at Hartwell, but everybody used them anyway. There was a little space behind some bushes by the athletic fields where kids hid from teachers while they made calls.

There were eight or ten kids—all of them girls—talking furtively on their phones when Daley got there. Everyone was squatting down so they couldn't be seen from any of the buildings. It looked like a bunch of girls peeing in the woods. Daley looked around to see if any teachers were watching, then squatted down and dialed.

"Hi, Gwen?"

"What's up, Daley?" her stepmother said.

"Just checking to see if you had managed to get hold of Ranger Mike about bringing the monkey out to the assembly this week."

"He's on for ten o'clock."

"Yay!"

NINE

That afternoon after school, Jackson walked into the house. Elaine was sitting in her La-Z-Boy chair watching soap operas. Tre and Davion were jumping up and down on the couch.

Jackson didn't say anything to anyone, just started walking back toward his room.

His foster mother switched off the TV and tossed the remote on the coffee table. "Don't I rate a 'Hello, Elaine?'" she said.

"Hello, Elaine," Jackson said, without enthusiasm. He still felt weird here, like he had to tiptoe the whole time, try not to take up any space. He went back to his room, got his books, and then came back out to the living room.

Elaine was standing in the doorway. "And where are you going?" she said. There was something in the tone of her voice, like she was angry with him.

"Library," he said.

She stood there with her hands on her hips. "I don't think so, young man," she said.

He looked at her, annoyed. What was she getting all mad about?

"Don't you take that attitude with me!" she said.

"What's the problem?"

"The problem?" She gave him a wincing smile. "The problem is that I went to the market yesterday with Tre and Davion. When I was done, I drove by the library. And guess what?"

Jackson didn't say anything.

"That's right. You weren't there."

"I did all my homework."

"That's not the point. You told me you were going to the library. You lied to me."

Jackson sighed loudly.

"Are you hanging out with those hoodlums from your old high school?"

Jackson didn't answer.

Tre and Davion were still bouncing up and down on the couch. "Jackson's in trouble!" they sang. "Jackson's in trouble!"

Jackson felt like he was in prison. He didn't know how much more of this he could take. Back when he'd been living with his mother, he'd been able to come and go whenever he wanted. His life with her hadn't exactly been idyllic—but at least he got to do what he wanted.

"I gotta go," he said.

"I don't think so," Elaine said.

"Please." He pushed past her, out the door.

"You get back here!"

He walked down the street. A man was watering his lawn, cheating on the water rationing.

"I'll call your caseworker at Social Services!" his foster mother yelled. "I'll send you back so fast it'll make your head spin."

The man who was watering his lawn gave Jackson a dirty look.

"What are you looking at?" Jackson said.

The man looked off into the distance like he hadn't heard a thing.

"You come back here!" Elaine yelled again.

Jackson just kept walking.

TEN

Taylor's Lexus screeched up to the curb outside Nathan's house. Taylor didn't seem to be able to stop without making large amounts of noise. As Nathan walked to the door, she blew the horn.

"Is she incapable of climbing out of her vehicle and knocking on the door like a normal person?" Nathan's mother said.

Nathan kissed her on the cheek. "Bye, Mom."

She waggled her index finger in his face. "Someday I'm gonna die and then you'll finally appreciate me."

Nathan laughed and started out the door.

His mother followed him out the door. "Where are you going?" she called after him.

"Rodeo Drive," Nathan called back to her. Rodeo Drive was the fanciest shopping area in Los Angeles, where all the big designers had boutiques. "She's got some kind of video shoot or something and she wants to get some clothes for it."

Taylor's head poked up out of the sunroof in her car. She waved. "Hi, Mrs. McHugh. I *love* what you did to your hair!"

Then she disappeared.

Nathan jumped in the car, feeling a mix of nervousness and excitement. Taylor seemed to have gotten over her big fit from the other day. If she stayed in a good mood, they could have some fun. She stomped on the gas and the car screeched out into the street, then bumped up onto the curb and back onto the road, narrowly missing the mailbox. Taylor was kind of a bad driver.

"Oops," she said.

"You would be doing me a big favor if you came up and knocked next time," Nathan said, tentatively, not wanting to start a fight, "instead of just blowing the horn."

"It's just I'm in a hurry. I've got an appointment at four fifteen."

"An appointment? To go shopping?"

Taylor looked at him. "No, I'm getting my legs waxed."

"You're what?"

"I'm getting my legs waxed. Everybody knows you can't go shopping on Rodeo Drive without—" She swerved on the road, missing the bumper of a dump truck by about two feet.

Nathan covered his head with his arms.

"Very funny." Taylor looked at him through narrowed eyes. "Hey, you don't *have* to come."

"No, no," Nathan said. "This is gonna be fun." Nathan was not a hundred percent sure what leg waxing was. But he didn't want to come off like a dope, so he didn't ask. Whatever it was, it involved stopping at a salon where she immediately went off into some back room, leaving him to sit around in the waiting room. What he'd had in mind was walking around with Taylor, joking around, looking in shop windows, having fun. After a few minutes of sitting there leafing sheepishly through fashion magazines, Nathan was starting to wish he'd stayed home and played video games or something.

For a while Nathan tried to read the magazines, but it was so boring (*Who* cares *what the hot color for summer is?*) that after a while he just sat and watched people walking up and down Rodeo Drive. It was mostly tourists and women who looked like Taylor's mother. Taylor's mother wore lots of gold jewelry and had had about three face-lifts already—even though she wasn't even that old.

Finally Taylor came out and spun around, making her skirt flare out around her legs. "Well?"

She looked pretty much exactly the same as she had an hour earlier. Which was great, of course. Nathan knew he had to sound enthusiastic. "Yeah!" Nathan said. "Right on!"

Taylor gave her dad's credit card to the woman in the skimpy outfit at the front desk. The woman didn't say how much it cost, but Nathan looked over Taylor's shoulder and saw that the register said $225. He couldn't believe it. Taylor's dad was supposedly one of the ten richest guys in California, so it wasn't like the money meant anything to her. But still. This just seemed like throwing money away.

Taylor seemed to be in a very good mood as they walked out onto the street. "This way," she said. They held hands as they walked down the street. Now this was more like it! *Walking down Rodeo Drive with a beautiful girl—what could be better?* But then after about a block Taylor turned into a store that said DA COSTA in teeny-weeny little silver letters on the window. It was like the idea was that if you didn't already know what was there, then they didn't want you coming there in the first place.

A man with a short beard and a suit coat worn over a T-shirt came out. "Sweetness!" he said with some kind of vaguely European accent. "Look at *you!*"

Then he and Taylor kissed each other on both cheeks. Nathan hoped the guy wouldn't try that on him. But as it turned out, he didn't have anything to worry about. The guy with the beard totally ignored him.

"I have something I've been saving for you, sweetness!" the bearded man said. "Only one!

Just for you!" He laced his fingers into Taylor's and dragged her into the back of the store.

"Great," Nathan said. Once again he was alone in foreign territory. He slumped down in a chair, then put his head in his hands. He felt really out of place here. This wasn't the kind of place that kids shopped. Not kids like him, anyway. It wasn't like his parents were poor or anything. But if they wanted to buy clothes, they went to Target or the mall or whatever.

Taylor's parents, on the other hand, were totally loaded. Her dad was this big real estate guy who was, like, seventy years old and was always flying all over the world doing deals.

After a minute, Nathan heard footsteps. He looked up and found a tall, thin man with ruffled sleeves and very carefully styled hair looking down disapprovingly at him.

"May I help you, sir?" the man said in a chilly voice.

"I'm just waiting for my girlfriend."

The man with the ruffled sleeves gave him a cold smile. "This is not a hotel lobby, young man."

Nathan pointed toward the back of the store. "Her name's Taylor Hagan. She went back there with that other guy?"

"Oh!" The man with the ruffled sleeves put his hand up to his mouth and widened his eyes theatrically. "You're Taylor's little friend! She's always talking about you. I'm so sorry! You know how it is, we're always getting these people in here who just want to be able to say they spent the afternoon at da Costa. It's so dreary!"

"Yeah," Nathan said. "I bet."

"May I get you a beverage?"

"Huh?" Nathan felt confused for a second. "Oh. Nah, I'm fine."

"I'm Jimmy!" The ruffle guy put out his hand to shake, crooking his fingers so it wasn't really possible to grab his whole hand. Nathan shook the man's fingers. It felt like he was shaking a handful of noodles. "Would you like me to show you the collection?"

Nathan blinked. "Uh . . . the collection?"

"Men's."

"Oh. You have guys' clothes here?"

The man with the ruffled sleeves seemed a little put out at this question. "My gosh! What kind of question is that?"

Just as Nathan was trying to figure out whether he wanted to look at clothes or not, a little bell tinkled and the door opened. Nathan was surprised to see another kid from his school, Eric McGorrill, walk in. As usual, Eric was wearing this little straw hat that he seemed to think made him look extremely cool.

"Dude!" Eric said, spotting Nathan.

"What's up?" Nathan said. Eric wasn't really a good friend of his or anything.

"Just doing a little shopping," Eric said. He turned to the man with the ruffled sleeves and said,

"Hey, bro, where are your shirts?"

"Follow me," the attendant said. Nathan stood up and followed the man and Eric up a flight of stairs to a sort of loft above the main store.

"So," Eric said. "You here with Taylor?"

"Uh-huh." Nathan was a little surprised to see Eric here. Eric didn't seem like the designer shirt kind of guy.

"Cool," Eric said. "How's the running-for-president thing going?"

"Great!" Nathan said. He was working hard to sound positive anytime anybody asked him about the election.

Eric squinted at him thoughtfully. "My perception? You're in a little trouble right now."

"Oh?"

"Daley's real organized," Eric said. "She's got a lot of momentum."

"She's got a crapload of posters, is what she's got."

Eric cracked up like Nathan was the funniest guy ever. "Tell you what you need, bro—"

The attendant interrupted. "Here's fall. There's some summer left, but not much."

Fall clothes? Nathan thought. Here it was, barely even summer. He felt like telling the guy with the noodley hands that they'd sell more clothes if they got their seasons right.

"Yeah, I'm definitely looking more for summer," Eric said. "Something kind of beach, you know? Beach, but not *beach* beach, you know what I mean?"

"I know *exactly*," the attendant said. He held up a T-shirt made of some kind of dull, orangey cloth that looked like it had come out of a dumpster. "Hm? Yes?"

"Oh, right on," Eric said. "How much is that?"

"Five, I think."

"Five dollars?" Eric said.

The attendant gave him his cool smile. "Hundred."

Nathan knew they sold stuff around here for a lot of money. But five hundred bucks? For a thing that looked like it had been used to mop up spilled orange juice?

Eric blinked, then grinned at the attendant. "Hey, bro, I had you, huh?" He jabbed his elbow into Nathan's ribs. "He thought I was serious."

The attendant's smile warmed only slightly.

"Why don't you take it down front and wrap it up," Eric said. "I'll pick it up when I leave."

"Super," the guy with the noodley hands said.

The two boys watched the attendant clatter down the stairs.

"Are you *serious*?" Nathan said. "You're really gonna pay five hundred bucks for that?"

"You must be kidding," Eric said. "I wouldn't wipe my dog's butt with that ugly thing." He laughed loudly.

Nathan couldn't help laughing, too.

"Yeah," Eric said. "I'll tell you what your campaign needs."

"What?"

He lowered his voice and leaned toward Nathan. "Dirty tricks."

"Dirty tricks?"

"Yeah, you know, Daley needs to be taken down a notch or two."

"Like . . . how?" Nathan figured the guy was blowing smoke, just making conversation. Eric was one of those guys who was always trying to shock people. But it couldn't hurt to get some new ideas.

"Well, see, that's where you want to *not* be going. Because if something happened and you knew about it? Hey, then it's on you. Right? Honor code violation, all that crapola? But if you don't know, then you got what they call plausible deniability."

"Plausible *what*?"

"Plausible deniability. It means you can say, 'I don't know a thing!' And you won't be lying. Because you *don't* know a thing."

Nathan frowned. "What—are you like . . . offering to do something like that for me?"

"For, oh, say, a hundred bucks? Yeah, I'd consider it."

Nathan felt unsettled. Was Eric joking? He was the kind of guy that you never really knew if he was serious or not. "That's not the kind of thing I'd do."

Eric jostled him so he stumbled into a rack of suits, then laughed loudly. "Dude! I can't believe you thought I was serious." While Nathan was extricating himself from the rack of clothes, Eric pointed down to the ground floor. "Hey, look, there's Taylor!"

Taylor was wearing a pair of frayed jeans and a green tank top with little da Costa logos embroidered on it in silver thread. She turned around and struck a couple of poses. Nathan had to admit, she looked pretty great. *If a ruined T-shirt cost five hundred dollars,* Nathan wondered, *how much would those crummy old jeans go for? A thousand?*

"Man," Eric called, "you look killer!"

Taylor looked at him blankly. "What are *you* doing here?"

"You know. Chillin'," he said blithely. "Picking up a few last things for the beach."

At which point Nathan started to wonder: Seriously, what *was* Eric doing there? Had he followed them there, or what? He obviously wasn't there to go shopping. And if he had followed them, why? The whole thing was weird.

Taylor disappeared into the back again.

As soon as she was gone, Eric started tiptoeing toward the door in an exaggerated way, a big smirk on his face. When he'd gotten to the door, he paused, turned, pointed his index finger at Nathan.

"Plausible deniability, bro," he said, winking. "Plausible deniability."

Then he was gone.

Weird, Nathan thought. *Very weird.*

Eric left the fancy store and hiked back down to where his mom's car was parked. He had borrowed the keys that afternoon and driven around randomly for a while. Well, not really randomly. He had sort of cruised by Taylor's house once or twice. Actually . . . a bunch of times. And then when she drove off, he had followed her.

He couldn't come up with any reasonable excuse for just "happening" to walk into the spa she had gone to. So he'd had to kill time until she and Nathan went over to that other store. Then he'd followed them in, just to get close to Taylor. And to do a little recon. He could feel a plan building in the back of his mind. But it hadn't quite firmed up yet.

Eric had a crush on Taylor. A really stupid, pointless, idiotic crush. Because there was no way Eric and Taylor would ever get together. Not at school, anyway. First off, she was, like, the prettiest girl in the class, and therefore way out of his league. And second, she had a boyfriend. Nathan. Mr. Nice Guy. Mr. Class President. Mr. Football.

There wasn't much he could do about the first problem. She wasn't going to get ugly and he wasn't going to turn into a really cool jock. But Mr. Nice Guy? Where was it written that Mr. Nice Guy was Taylor's boyfriend for life? Nowhere. Yeah, that's right. Mr. Nice Guy could be eliminated. Right?

It hadn't really struck him how that might work, though—not until he was standing there talking to Nathan in the shop. And then it was like—*bam!*—lightning had struck.

There it was in his head. An entire plan had crystallized. Yes!

In less than two weeks the camping club was flying to Palau. If Eric could nudge good ol' Nathan out of the box, then he and Taylor would be thrown together in a very—shall we say—*intimate setting?* Five thousand miles from home on some dinky little tropical paradise? Hey, anything could happen! Huh? Yes? Correct?

Very much correct.

But first? He had to get rid of Nathan. And now he thought he knew exactly how to do it.

ELEVEN

A NEW GYM. NEXT YEAR.
THAT'S A PROMISE!
NATHAN FOR PREZ.

"So that's it," Melissa said, taping the last poster on the wall.

"That totally rocks!" Nathan said, stepping back to look. "That looks as good as Daley's posters any day of the week."

Melissa felt a flush of happiness. She had been up until eleven the previous night printing up posters, neglecting her homework. Once she'd gotten started, she'd gotten a little carried away and printed out about a bazillion of them. Then, starting at seven o'clock in the morning, she and Nathan had been taping them up all over the school.

They were everywhere, completely unavoidable. Daley was going to freak.

Kids had started arriving a few minutes earlier. As Melissa and Nathan were admiring the poster, a couple of girls in cheerleader uniforms came up. One of the cheerleaders, Abby Fujimoto, said, "Wow! You're gonna get a new gym! It's about time."

"Cool, huh?" Nathan said. Nathan was beaming, suddenly back to his normal, optimistic self.

"Last year didn't Dr. Shook say we couldn't afford to get one?" Abby said.

"Well, yeah," Nathan said. "But, look, if everybody gets behind it, we could do it. I'm going to form a committee composed of staff, students, and parents. Then it's just a question of raising the money."

"Oh. Wow." One of the other cheerleaders, Courtney Rogers, put her hand on Nathan's arm. "I am so impressed."

"Hey . . ." Nathan shrugged modestly.

Melissa suddenly felt invisible with all the cheerleaders around. But what could she do?

Daley was feeling intensely irritated. All morning people had been coming up to her and saying, "Did you hear about Nathan? He's going to get us a new gym."

Yeah, right, Daley kept thinking. *Like that's really going to happen.* A new gym would cost millions of dollars. It wasn't like a class president could magically wave a wand and make a gym appear.

At lunch she found herself in line next to Nathan. She turned and gave him a superior smile. "A new gym?" she said. "Why not fly the entire junior class to the moon while you're at it?"

Nathan didn't seem to be bothered. "Look, you chose to go with a bunch of little dinky issues," he said. "Cool. Hey, that's one way to fly. I just happen to be more of a big picture guy."

"How comforting," Daley said. "So I hear you're making a video as your summer project. Ten rules for how to get elected president of the class?"

Nathan nodded. "Something like that."

"They'll have a hard time taking it seriously when you lose, don't you think?"

Nathan smiled. "Yeah, but that's not gonna happen."

Daley snorted, then turned to the food server. "I'll have the vegetarian lunch, Mrs. Gordon."

Nathan gave a disgusted look at the gray, jelly-like squares of tofu that Mrs. Gordon was piling onto Daley's tray. "Hi, Mrs. Gordon. Hamburger and fries for me."

"So, you want to share any of your ten rules with me?" Daley said.

"Rule seven," Nathan said. "Tofu is for losers."

TWELVE

"**D**efinitely not."

Nathan blinked. Dr. Shook, the headmaster, smiled apologetically at him.

"I mean, hey, Nathan, I applaud your ambition. We're all about encouraging visionary thinking here at Hartwell. But the school's capital budget is all worked out five years in advance. A new gym is just not going to happen right now."

Nathan felt a stab of dejection. Couldn't *anything* go right in this campaign? "But it's . . . possible. Right?"

Dr. Shook smiled brightly and nodded enthusiastically. "Actually? No."

Nathan wondered why he was nodding his head. It was always like that at Hartwell. They were afraid of squashing your poor little ego, so they were always saying things in really positive ways. And then when they dropped the bad news on you, you almost wished they'd been mean about it. That way, you could at least salvage a little dignity by hating them.

"Like, could you put a percentage on that, Dr. Shook?" Nathan was grasping at straws. "Like, there's a ten percent chance we could do it? Twenty percent? Fifty percent?"

Dr. Shook was still nodding and grinning away. "Pretty much zero possibility."

"But—"

"We have an honor code here, Nathan." Dr. Shook sat next to him, put his arm around Nathan's shoulder. "It's a very treasured part of the Hartwell experience."

"Uh-huh."

Dr. Shook paused for a moment, like he was waiting for Nathan to say something. When Nathan didn't speak, Dr. Shook said, "You see where I'm going, don't you, Nathan?"

Nathan had a bad feeling that he did. "I'm not sure."

"Well, if a person running for office makes a campaign promise that's just not possible for him to fulfill, then it's not really ethical to make that promise. Right?"

"I guess. But—"

"Good!" Dr. Shook clapped him on the shoulder. "Then you should be able to get all the posters taken down by, what, the end of sixth period?"

Nathan felt a surge of outrage. This wasn't fair! Melissa had knocked herself out printing them, and then he'd spent all morning putting up the posters. And now—

"You're a great kid, Nathan! Knew you'd understand."

Dr. Shook gave him another big exasperatingly hearty slap on the shoulder, put in the ear buds of his iPod, and walked away bopping his head to some corny old song from the sixties.

THIRTEEN

RULE FOUR:
DO SOMETHING
DRAMATIC

Nathan's ears were burning the entire time he was taking his posters down. Talk about feeling like a loser! This was the *worst*.

He had taken the last poster down when he heard someone come up behind him and say, "Dude! What you doing?"

He turned and there was Eric McGorrill. "Boy," Nathan said, "that guy at the store got real pissy after you snuck out without buying that shirt."

Eric laughed. "I bet. But where do they get off charging five bills for a T-shirt, anyway?" He looked up and down the hallway. "What happened to all your posters?"

"Uh. Had to take them down."

"Why?"

Nathan explained that Dr. Shook had given

him this whole honor code routine.

"Oh, that's so not fair," Eric said. The bell rang for seventh period. "Gotta roll."

"See you."

Eric had walked about ten feet when he turned and said, "Hundred bucks, bro. Daley will never know what hit her. Think about it."

Then he was gone.

When Jackson got home that night, he saw a pale blue Chevy with no hubcaps and a state seal on the side parked at the curb. His heart sank. In all the time he'd been dealing with the people from CDSS, he'd never gotten any good news from them. They'd brought him the news when his mother had been arrested. They'd told him he was going to be placed in foster care. And the Chevy probably belonged to that Mr. Rosenthal guy, the one who seemed to have it in for him.

When Jackson went inside, Elaine and the caseworker were sitting in the formal living room, the one that Elaine never used, with all the plastic covers on the furniture. Mr. Rosenthal smiled broadly as Jackson walked in. "There's the man of the hour!" he said with a bunch of fake enthusiasm.

"What now?" Jackson said. He figured he was going to get the news now: Elaine was going to kick him out for lying about going to the library and then walking away from her the previous day.

Mr. Rosenthal was a small, pudgy man with tiny, pudgy hands, like the hands of a doll. He frowned. "Hey, hey, hey! Why the attitude? We've got good news."

Jackson stood in the doorway.

"Sit," Mr. Rosenthal said.

Jackson remained standing.

"Look, Elaine did mention she had some behavior concerns. And we'll talk about that in a little bit. But that's not why I'm here." He leaned over and slapped the plastic-covered couch. "C'mon! Sit. It won't kill you."

Jackson slumped down on the couch.

"Just got news," Mr. Rosenthal said. "My supervisor has approved you to go on this trip to—" He scrabbled around, opened a folder, looking for something.

"Palau," Jackson said.

"Palau!" Mr. Rosenthal closed the folder. "That's it. As you know, you're under administrative guidance. That's kind of like the juvenile equivalent of probation. Means you have to have permission to leave the state."

Jackson gave him a look which he hoped conveyed the question: *How dumb do you think I am that you have to explain all this stuff?*

"Anyway, Jackson, I believe in you. But I got to tell you, I had to pull in quite a few favors with my supervisor to get him to sign off on this."

Yeah, right. He'd probably been fighting to keep Jackson from going. Jackson kept waiting for the bad news.

"What, you aren't gonna thank me?"

"Thanks," Jackson said. "What's the bad news?"

Mr. Rosenthal studied Jackson's face. He was still smiling, but there was something kind of queasy about it. Finally he turned to Elaine and said, "Ms. Berkhalter, you mind letting me and Jackson have a little heart-to-heart?"

"Oh, sure!" she said, blinking. She left the room, went out to the kitchen.

Mr. Rosenthal smiled for a while and then said, "Jackson, what are you doing?"

"What?"

At long last Mr. Rosenthal's smile faded. He didn't look scary or even mean. He mostly just looked tired. "Son, look, you're a really bright kid. You've come from a really crummy family situation. Your grades are excellent. Your attendance is good. Your scores are off the charts. But there's a reason the department took you out of that neighborhood. You were running with some bad people."

Jackson just kept looking at him.

"I'm going to ask you a direct question. When you go sneaking off in the afternoons, where are you going?"

"Why is that your business?"

Mr. Rosenthal shook his head sadly. "Are you running with your little gangster buddies from back at Chavez?"

"No."

"Then what *are* you doing?"

Jackson was pretty sure he was going to make Honor Society this semester at Hartwell. And Hartwell was, like, ten times harder than Chavez. He didn't see why he needed to account for every minute of his time.

Jackson shrugged.

"I'm asking you, flat out. Where are you going?"

"It's personal."

"What, you got a girlfriend? You going skateboarding? Playing in a rock band?" Brief pause. "Stealing cars?"

Jackson didn't answer.

Mr. Rosenthal drummed his fingers on the table in front of him. "I'm going to check with the principal—excuse me, the *headmaster*—over at Hartwell." He curled his lips sarcastically. "If your grades are good and your behavior is up to snuff at your hoity-toity new school—hey, I'm not going to stick it to you."

Mr. Rosenthal leaned forward, pointed his finger at Jackson's face. "But let me remind you, kiddo. You're on thin ice. I can snatch you out of here on ten minutes notice and send you up to the high security juvenile detention facility up in Paso Robles. Paso Robles, that's twenty-four-seven inside a locked cage. A locked cage full of animals."

Jackson didn't even blink.

"One mistake, one incident at school, one sign that you're hanging out with your little friends from Chavez again"—Mr. Rosenthal snapped his fingers—"and you're gone."

"Can I go now?" Jackson said.

FOURTEEN

The next morning there was a student assembly. Once a month, the student body got together in the auditorium and a speaker—usually boring—would come out and give a speech.

Today's speech was by this washed-up actress named Nell Robbins who used to be on a show about a talking dog named Bertrand Russell Terrier. The aging dog was there, too.

Daley, however, was not watching the speech. She was standing in the parking lot looking at her watch and waiting for the person from the zoo to show up with the monkey. They were supposed to be there at nine thirty. But now it was nine fifty-five—halfway through the speech.

And nobody from the zoo had showed up.

Dr. Shook came out and looked around. "Still no monkey, huh?" he said.

Daley pursed her lips. "This is so infuriating."

"It'll be fine. We can squeeze you in at the end of the assembly."

Daley was about to go back inside when the Zoomobile—a big RV with pictures of animals painted on the side—swung into the parking lot.

"Thank goodness," Daley said.

It turned out that the event at Hartwell was not important enough to the zoo for them to send Ranger Mike. Instead they had sent a skinny young man who looked like he was barely out of high school himself. He wore a baggy zookeeper costume composed of a safari jacket, Bermuda shorts, and high green socks that had fallen down and bunched up around his ankles. The badge on his chest said: HELLO I'M DARREN—TRAINEE. "Um," Darren said to Daley as he lugged the monkey's cage through the door that led onto the stage of the auditorium, "I'm a little n-n-n-nervous." He had a strong stutter. "This is the first time I've been out of the zoo with an animal."

"It's just a little monkey," Daley said. "It'll be fine." The cute monkey was curled up, munching on a carrot. Daley put her finger in the cage.

"I wouldn't n-n-necessarily do that," the zookeeper named Darren said. "Monkeys are kind of high strung."

The monkey reached out and grabbed Daley's

hand. Daley jumped. But the monkey just leaned forward and started licking her finger.

"Oh, look at him," she said. "He's so sweet! Can I hold him?"

"Um. I was kinda thinking of l-l-leaving him in the cage."

"Leaving him in the cage!" Daley said. "That defeats the whole purpose of bringing him, don't you think?"

Darren smiled weakly. "Well, I guess it couldn't hurt. I'll take him out and then see how he reacts to you."

They reached the stage curtain and Darren set down the monkey's cage, still out of view of the students in the audience. Dr. Shook followed them.

"Wait here," Dr. Shook said. He crossed over to the podium. The actress, Nell Robbins, stopped talking and Dr. Shook spoke into the microphone. "How about a big hand for Nell Robbins!"

Darren bent over, opened the cage, pulled out the monkey, and lifted him up. The monkey's big eyes looked sweetly into Daley's face. She reached out a finger and gently rubbed his nose. The monkey nuzzled her hand.

"Seems like he likes you," Darren said. "Let's see how he does."

He placed the monkey in Daley's arms. The little monkey looked nervously around for a second, but then seemed to relax. It curled up in her arms, cuddling into her like a baby.

"Okay," Dr. Shook said. "One last thing before we let you go." There were groans from the crowd. "Daley Marin, a member of the camping club, has a brief announcement."

Daley walked out with the monkey cradled in her arms.

Kids immediately saw the monkey and squealed, "Ohhh, look!" and "It's so cute!" and "That's so sweet!" and "Check out the monkey!"

"Hi, everybody," Daley said into the microphone. "Isn't this little guy cute?"

The monkey raised its head and looked around. The audience roared. It was obvious people were much more interested in the monkey than they were in Nell Robbins.

Daley started explaining about the contest and how it was for the benefit of the camping club's trip to Palau.

"How do we get tickets?" a girl in the front row yelled.

"Yeah," another said, "I want one."

"Me too. Me too!"

"I want five!"

Daley held up one hand. "We'll have a table out by the cafeteria at lunchtime."

From the wings, Darren suddenly began motioning frantically at her.

She looked at him curiously. "What?"

"Uh . . ." he was pointing at something on the floor.

"What?"

"Most monkeys don't like d-d-duh—" Darren had the sort of stutter that pretty much shut down his ability to talk sometimes.

"I'm sorry?"

Darren kept jabbing his finger. "D—" he said. "Duh—"

"Duh?"

"Duh! Duh!" Jabbing his finger at something.

Daley looked around. What was he pointing at? Nell Robbins's shoes? Something on the floor?

"—Duh-dogs!"

Suddenly the monkey let out an outrageously loud scream and grabbed Daley's hair. She screamed.

The TV dog, Bertrand, had spent the entire speech lying on the stage. But as soon as it saw the monkey, it started barking and lunging at Daley. Nell Robbins hauled on its leash, but not in time to stop the little Jack Russell terrier from slamming into Daley's leg. Daley stumbled backward.

The monkey howled again and jumped up on Daley's head, trying to put as much distance between itself and the dog as possible. Its tail wrapped around her head, covering her eyes so she couldn't see. She flailed wildly, trying to dislodge the panicked monkey.

"Nuh-nuh-no!" shouted Darren. "You'll scare the monkey!"

She could hear kids in the crowd laughing and hooting. She was mortified. This whole thing was turning out to be a nightmare. Daley blundered around blindly. Suddenly the monkey moved its tail and she could see again. She felt the monkey standing up straight on top of her head, its tiny feet yanking on her hair.

"Ow!" she howled. "Get it off me!"

Dr. Shook lunged nervously for the monkey. The monkey, however, had a different idea. It vaulted off her head and onto the podium, where it arched its back and raised its hands in the air.

"Watch out!" Darren yelled. "When they get nervous the tend to p-puh—"

The monkey peed.

A stream of pee soared through the air, hitting the aging actress Nell Robbins right in the face.

Every kid in the room was dying laughing. In the front row, Eric had literally fallen out of his chair and was lying on the ground holding his sides.

Daley felt rooted to the spot. What would the crazy monkey do next?

Suddenly Nathan vaulted over the first row of chairs, jumped onto the stage, and grabbed the monkey, holding it out at arm's length so it couldn't pee on him.

The crowd broke into wild applause. *Of all people,* Daley thought, *it had to be Nathan.*

Nathan grinned and held the monkey up in the air like a trophy. The monkey, too, held up its arms—as though it had just won a gold medal in the Olympics—its head thrown back, its fur sticking up in little spikes, its tiny teeth bared, howling at the top of its lungs.

"Woooo!" Kids were stamping and cheering and laughing.

Daley had never felt so stupid in her entire life. She turned and ran off the stage.

Rule Four? Look, people like excitement. People like a president who'll lead from the front. When you see a chance to draw a little positive attention to yourself—do it.

Some people—I'm not pointing fingers here— but some people aren't comfortable with excitement. They want everything controlled and predictable. And that's okay. That's good for being valedictorian or something like that. But a president needs to be able to go with the flow, change directions, roll with the punches, go down swingin'. Well, no, not that last one. But you see what I mean? You have to be able to, uh, seize victory from the jaws of defeat.

A monkey jumps on your head? Don't scream and get all freaked out. Hey, just do something. Grab the monkey. That's leadership.

Rule Four: Do something dramatic.

Daley spent the first five minutes of fourth period hiding in the bathroom. This was surely the most embarrassing thing that had happened to her in her entire life.

And the timing couldn't be worse. Less than a week before the election! She'd figured out all the issues that people in her grade wanted addressed by student council, she'd done great posters, she'd organized a bunch of kids to help her, and her opponent was doing a terrible job in just about every way. She had the momentum. She had respect. Everything was going great.

And suddenly she was the laughingstock of the entire school. The big joke. All her hard work, out the window.

People would be telling stories about this when they came back for their fiftieth reunion, leaning on their canes and breathing out of oxygen bottles. "Remember that time the monkey jumped on Daley's head and then peed on that washed-up actress?" One of her aging classmates would probably die of a stroke from laughing so hard.

And the election? Forget it. Forget being class president. Forget Harvard. Forget all her big dreams about being a famous scientist and curing childhood leukemia and all that junk. Stupid! Stupid! Stupid!

She looked at her watch. She was supposed to be sitting at the table outside the cafeteria selling raffle tickets to name the monkey. Oh God, oh God, oh God. Nobody would buy a ticket now! She'd single-handedly ruined any chance they had of going to Palau.

Now it was going to be back to Nathan and his stupid car wash.

She stood up straight, walked out the door of the bathroom. Three boys from the ninth grade turned and stared at her, not even trying to suppress their giggling. She gave them the official Daley Marin Evil Eye.

"Ooo! Ooo! Ooo!" one boy yelled, making monkey noises while he danced up and down and scratched one of his underarms. His friends seemed to think he was a comic genius.

Everybody in the hallway started staring and pointing and howling like monkeys. She glared at them. The howling and the laughter got louder.

Daley turned around. *I think I'll just go back in the bathroom and stay there forever.*

"Daley!" a voice called. "Wait! Daley!"

Daley hurried back into the bathroom and into a stall, slammed the door shut.

Footsteps followed her into the bathroom.

"Daley!" She recognized the nervous voice of Jory Twist, one of the girls in the camping club. Daley vaguely recalled that they were scheduled to sit together to sell raffle tickets.

Jory's footsteps followed Daley to the stall. She started banging on the door.

"Daley! Daley! Hurry! Please! We have a terrible problem!"

Daley felt like saying: *You* have a problem?

Eric was wearing his shades and hanging out by the water fountain in the hallway when the new guy, Jackson, walked by.

"S'up, bro?" Eric said, raising his chin a little.

The new guy looked at him coolly but didn't answer.

Eric watched him as he walked on down the hallway. *Who put the bug up* that *guy's behind?*

Jackson stopped at his locker, opened it up, and looked up and down the hallway like he was worried somebody was watching him. Eric kept his head angled so that it seemed like he wasn't looking at Jackson. But, in fact, he had his eyeballs swiveled behind his sunglasses, watching Jackson the whole time.

Jackson grabbed something out of his locker and stuffed it under his shirt. It was about a foot long and had a metallic gleam. *And what is* that? Eric thought. There were stories going around the school that Jackson was, like, some kind of gang-banger or something. You had to wonder why Dr. Shook would admit a guy like that. Didn't really seem to fit in around here.

Whatever it was that Jackson had stuck under his shirt, it was hidden now. He seemed real suspicious, though—scanning the hallway before heading back toward the Art Annex.

The Art Annex? Strange. Only the weirdo goth-type kids hung out there.

Eric casually ambled off in the same direction as Jackson, hands in his pockets. After Jackson turned the corner at the end of the hall, Eric hustled quickly and silently down to the door leading out to the Art Annex.

He got there just in time to see Jackson look suspiciously around him, then ease the door open to the graphic arts room.

Eric tiptoed outside and over to the door of the graphic arts room. Peering through the small window, he saw Jackson hunched over the computer workstation in the back, next to the scanner and the big poster printer. There was still one poster lying on the floor next to it, saying how Nathan McHugh was going to get a gym built next year.

And what was that thing in Jackson's hand? *Whoa! Check it out!*

Some ideas started popping into Eric's head.

"Please! Daley!" Jory kept banging on the door of the bathroom stall.

Finally Daley yanked the door open. "What!"

"Sorry! Sorry!" Jory said. "It's just . . . there's a problem."

"I thought you were supposed to be selling raffle tickets right now."

"That's the problem!"

"What, yeah, the monkey peed on that lady and jumped on my head and now I'm a big joke and nobody's gonna buy tickets for the raffle. Fine. Just leave me alone."

She tried to close the door but Jory held it open.

"Nooo!" Jory grabbed her sleeve, pulling impatiently on it. "You have to come!"

Daley sighed loudly. "Oh, for Pete's sake!"

She followed Jory out of the bathroom. Mercifully, everyone seemed to be in class or at lunch, so there was no one in the hall to make fun of her now.

They walked rapidly down toward the cafeteria. As they came around the corner, she saw a long line of kids standing by the far wall. The line stretched all the way around the corner.

"What is this?" Daley said.

"The monkey!" Jory said. "Everybody's gone crazy after what you did with the monkey."

Daley frowned.

Somebody spotted Daley and pointed at her. Then suddenly all the kids were running toward her. "I want to name the monkey!" one girl yelled.

"Can we get ten tickets?" another kid yelled.

People were laughing and shoving. "It's my monkey!"

"Dude, *I'm* naming it!"

"Bro, I'm naming it after you!"

"Oh, my God!" Daley said.

And then everybody burst into applause. "Way to go, Daley!" one of them yelled.

"Daley rocks!" another yelled.

They were crowding around her like she was a movie star or something.

Daley felt a huge sensation of relief sweeping through her. She couldn't believe it. This whole thing had somehow totally turned to her advantage. Now it was time to get things under control. She held up her hands. "All right, all right, all right, people!" she called, striding toward the table where the raffle tickets lay. "Back in line. Have your money in your hand. Cash only!"

Nathan was getting his lunch when he heard all the noise out in the hallway. He picked up his tray, walked to the door, and looked out.

He couldn't believe it. There must have been a hundred kids lined up to buy raffle tickets. And then all these kids started applauding when Daley appeared. Totally, totally ridiculous.

"Hey!" he called. "I'm the one who saved the monkey!"

But no one was listening.

Someone appeared at his elbow. Eric.

"I don't get it," Nathan said, shaking his head.

"I don't, either," Eric said, staring out at the mob of kids through his dark sunglasses. "You're the big hero and she's getting all the attention."

"That's what I'm saying."

They watched the kids clamoring and elbowing each other, waiting to get tickets.

"Dirty tricks, huh?" Nathan said.

"Hey, man, I was just joking. I'd never do anything like that."

"Yeah, oh, sure! Of course!" Nathan said. "Obviously!"

FIFTEEN

RULE FIVE:
NO DIRTY TRICKS

Daley was amazed. The crowd of raffle ticket buyers just kept surging forward. Pretty soon the metal money box they were using was full to the point of overflowing. Bills were actually spilling out on the floor.

"I'll be back in a second," Daley said. She ran into the lunch room and looked around until she saw a kid pulling his lunch out of a brown paper bag.

"Can I have that?" she said.

"Sure," he said.

"Vote Daley for Prez!" she said.

"I'll think about it," the boy said.

She ran back out the door, past Nathan and Eric, sat down at the table, and started transferring some of the excess bills into the paper bag.

"In all seriousness, though?" Eric said. He pointed across the hallway. "Look how Daley's working it. Science."

"Science?" Nathan said.

"The posters."

Nathan frowned, not getting what Eric was talking about. Above the table where Daley was selling raffle tickets were several of her posters, listing all the trivial little things she claimed she was going to do if she became president of the class.

"Remember how she had all these girls walking around with clipboards?" Eric said. "They were asking what people wanted. But they also asked you personal questions. Like, whether you played sports, or if you liked certain kinds of music, and all this stuff."

"So?"

"See, her campaign promises? They're not just a list of random junk. They're designed to appeal to every group in the school. Football jocks. Soccer team. Band geeks. Popular girls. Emos. Renaissance festival weirdos. Everybody."

"Huh."

"One issue per group."

Nathan saw it now. Boy, that *was* smart. He had totally missed that. "Maybe I should do a survey, too."

Eric shook his head. "Dude, that's a waste. She's already found the issues. You'd just look like some copycat."

"Yeah, I know. But I tried having like one big issue and it kinda . . . uh . . ."

"The Shookster hosed you."

"Right."

"See, what you need is—"

"Don't say dirty tricks again."

"Hey, that was a joke. I'm being serious now. What you need is a people strategy."

"Meaning what?"

"Look, you're not running for president of the United States. Nobody really cares what the student council does. C'mon! Everybody knows this is about all the kids in the class saying, 'Hey, you've got it together. You deserve to go to Harvard.' See, it's like the grand prize."

"Like a popularity contest."

"No. If it was *just* popularity, you'd beat Daley's pants off. But everybody knows she's little miss overachiever. Nah, what you need is to get your story out about how important this is to you. How deserving you are."

"How would I do that?"

"Okay, first, you need the story. You're the first kid in your family to go to college, overcoming big obstacles, yadda, yadda, yadda."

"Yeah, but everybody in my family's gone to college for, like, a hundred years."

Eric looked thoughtful. "Okay. Well, whatever.

You're gonna cure cancer."

"I believe Daley's already got that one. Remember, her mom died of cancer a few years ago? And so she's always telling people how she wants to find a cure for—"

Eric waved his hand impatiently. "Whatever. Point is, in your story, it's got to be like heroic little guy, man of destiny, overcoming all odds, all that crapola. You figure out the story."

"And then what? Write an article for the *Hartwellian*?"

"God, no! You'd look totally bogus and phony. Besides, I only have one rule in life. Always get somebody else to do the work."

Nathan looked at Eric blankly.

"Nathan! C'mon! Think! Point is, you need to find the people who are most likely to tell the story. Get the story out through them."

Nathan narrowed his eyes thoughtfully, trying to figure out where he was going with this.

"Dude! Popular girls. You got to spend a little quality time with all the most popular honeys in the school. Tell them your story. Big drama, you're such a deserving guy, if you don't make president, you're life's dreams and aspirations will be totally wrecked."

"And then what?"

"That's it. Tell your story. The popular girls are all like—*yip yip yip yip yip*. All they do is talk and talk and talk. Two days and everybody in the entire school will know why you and you alone deserve to be president of the class." He punched his palm. "Bam! You're there."

Nathan studied Eric's face, then grinned. "Man, you are a very smart guy. Thanks."

Taylor came around the corner and spotted Nathan.

Eric watched enviously as Taylor came up and started talking to Nathan about some fashion video thing. She didn't even look at Eric. He might as well have been invisible.

"Look, I gotta go," Nathan said. "Tell my story, huh? Very smart, Eric. Very smart." Then he put his arm around Taylor's shoulders, and the happy couple walked away.

Smarter than you know, bro, Eric thought as he watched them disappear into the crowd of students. *Smarter than you know.*

After lunch was over, Daley counted the cash in the box. It was close to two thousand dollars! She couldn't believe it. She felt exhausted and elated. She had been selling raffle tickets nonstop through both lunch periods. It didn't even occur to her until the bell for sixth period rang that she hadn't eaten anything.

Eventually the crowds thinned out as students made their way to their next class.

Daley put the money in a paper bag and set it on the floor next to the table. Then she stood up and said to Jory, "I'm going to grab a piece of fruit. Can you hold down the fort?"

"Sure," Jory said, opening her book bag. "I'll just eat my lunch here."

Daley went into the lunch room and picked up a banana and a couple of packs of crackers from the salad bar. There were a few students left. She made a point of speaking to each one of them, asking for their vote.

Then she went back into the corridor.

Jory was gone.

Daley frowned. The paper bag was gone, too. She assumed Jory had taken the money to the front office and given it to Mrs. Windsor. But it made her nervous.

As she was looking curiously at the table, the new guy, Jackson, walked by her. He was looking around furtively.

"Did you see Jory Twist as you came down that hallway?" Daley said.

"Down what hallway?"

She pointed in the direction of the hall that led out to the Art Annex.

"I didn't come that way."

Daley wrinkled her forehead. "I just saw you," she said.

Jackson frowned. "Well, I didn't see her."

"Do you even know who I'm talking about?"

Jackson looked at her blankly.

"Did you see a bag sitting by that table?"

"I gotta get to class," he said. Then he turned

and hurried off down the hallway.

Daley watched him go, wondering why he was acting so weird. Well, no matter. Jory was in music class with her. She'd get the money from her there.

Daley went to her locker, got her books, and walked across the school to Mr. O'Neal's classroom.

"Sorry I'm late," she said.

Mr. O'Neal was a tall blond man with a big overbite. "No problem," he said. "You must have been counting all that money you guys made today."

Daley smiled nervously, then sat down next to Jory and whispered, "Hey, can you give me the money? Or did you hand it in at the office?"

Jory looked at her curiously. "The what?"

"The money. What did you do with the raffle money?"

Jory looked at her quizzically. "I thought *you* had the money."

Daley felt her eyes widen, a wave of panic flashing through her. "Jory, I left the money with you! Why do you think I told you to hold down the fort until I came back?"

"But . . . Dr. Shook came by and told me I should go on to class. I didn't even know the money was—"

"Is there a problem, girls?" Mr. O'Neal said.

Daley felt her heart rise in her throat. She turned to look at Mr. O'Neal. For a minute she felt like she couldn't breathe.

SIXTEEN

Dr. Shook sat on the edge of his desk, frowning. Daley sat in the chair in front of him, feeling very small.

"How much are we talking?"

"One thousand, nine hundred and twenty dollars."

Dr. Shook's eyebrows went up. "Wow!"

"I don't know what could have happened! I wasn't gone for more than two minutes."

"Maybe Earl picked it up, thought it was trash." Earl was the janitor. Dr. Shook pulled out a walkie-talkie and said, "Earl. Could you come to my office?"

They waited in silence.

Shortly, the janitor walked in. He was an old, white-haired man who always had a big smile on his craggy face and wore a battered cowboy hat.

"What can I do you fer?" he said.

"Have you been cleaning up around the cafeteria today?"

Earl shook his head. "Naw, I been cleaning up the gym all morning."

"Daley here lost a paper bag that had some money in it. We were afraid it might have gotten thrown away."

"Not by me."

"Thanks, Earl," Dr. Shook said. "Didn't mean to hold you up."

The janitor left and Dr. Shook turned back toward Daley.

"Did you see anybody hanging around where the money was? Acting suspicious?"

Daley thought about it. "Well . . . Jackson walked by. He was acting a little . . . strange."

"Strange how?"

"Looking over his shoulder. He was coming from the direction of the Art Annex. But there aren't any classes going on there at lunch time. I don't know. He just seemed . . ."

Dr. Shook gave her a long look. "You realize this is a very serious thing."

"I'm not saying he stole the money. It's just . . . weird."

Dr. Shook crossed his arms. "I think we need to have a little chat with Mr. Jackson." He picked up the walkie-talkie. "You can go back to class, Daley."

Melissa and Nathan were sitting in the back of the Art Annex. Melissa was sketching Nathan. Unlike Nathan, she was really good at art—though she never seemed to realize how talented she was. Nathan, on the other hand, could barely draw a smiley face.

"He said I need a story," Nathan said, still thinking about what Eric had said. "He said people vote for who they think deserves it, not who they think will really do the most stuff in student council. So the idea would be that I need to come up with a story about what a deserving guy I am. Can you help me out?"

Melissa held up the thin piece of charcoal she was drawing with, studied his face, then drew some more. "What's wrong with 'I'm a nice guy and I'll do a good job'?"

"Eric said it needs to be specific. Like, 'I need this so I can get into Harvard so I can be this big scientist and cure cancer.'"

"Isn't that Daley's thing?"

"I'm just saying . . ."

"Huh. I guess I gotta think about it." Melissa scratched her face, leaving a black smudge on her cheek. "I know you're gonna think it's terrible . . ." She turned the picture around.

Nathan couldn't believe it. It was, like, the best picture he'd ever seen anybody draw. "Wow!" he said.

The guy in the picture—it was almost like looking in the mirror. Only . . . the guy in the picture looked kind of nervous.

Jackson sat down in the chair. Dr. Shook was standing, looking down at him. He had a poster of Jimi Hendrix on the wall behind his desk, and over by the book shelf he had a Gibson Les Paul electric guitar leaned up against a big, black amplifier. Jackson thought that was a weird thing for a principal to have in his office. Back at Chavez, Mrs. Eberly just had American flags and certificates and all this boring junk on the walls.

"How you doing, Jackson?" Dr. Shook said. He had a big smile on his face that Jackson didn't completely buy.

"Fine."

"Settling in okay?"

Jackson nodded.

"You know, something occurred to me today. You came in the middle of the year and I'm not sure that we ever really explained about our honor code here at Hartwell." He paused and seemed to be waiting for Jackson to say something. But Jackson just sat there, arms folded.

"See, Jackson, the honor code is a treasured part of our school. Maybe more important than academics. The core notion of our honor code is individual responsibility. Hey, let's face it— everybody does things now and then that they shouldn't. The honor code here says that the most important thing you can do is own up to your mistakes." Big smile. "You with me?"

Here it came, Jackson thought. Somebody must have ratted him out.

"It's about sharing values. It's about personal exploration and growth."

Yeah, yeah, yeah. Get on with it.

Dr. Shook gave a nervous laugh. "You're sitting there like a rock, pal. You with me on what I'm saying so far?"

Jackson nodded.

"Terrific. I bring it up because we had a little incident today and—ah—could be just an accident, an oversight, a mistake . . ."

Again, he seemed to be waiting for Jackson to chime in and say something. Jackson didn't play that game. *You got something to say, fine. Say it. Don't beat around the bush.*

"What I'm saying, Jackson, is that it didn't have to be malicious. If you did something and it was just a mistake? And you own up to it? And you have an explanation . . . that seems reasonable . . ." Dr. Shook spread his hands.

Jackson didn't move a muscle.

"Jackson?"

"Yes?"

Dr. Shook studied his face for a long time. "I don't know how it worked back at Chavez. But around here, this is a real open, safe environment. You know? We're all about dialogue here." He moved his hand back and forth in the air like he was drawing some kind of connection between them in the air. "You can talk here. Share. Be real. It's safe."

What in the world was this clown tripping about? Talking was *never* safe. Never. Every time you opened your mouth, it was an opportunity for somebody to jump down your throat.

"Jackson?" Dr. Shook seemed to be getting irritated now.

"Uh-huh."

"Do me a favor and read this." Dr. Shook handed Jackson a folded piece of paper.

Jackson unfolded the paper. On it was a message printed on a laser printer in large letters:

YOU SHOULD SEARCH CODY JACKSON'S LOCKER.

"I found this note shoved under my door when I came back from lunch today," Dr. Shook said. "Any idea why someone might have sent this to me?"

"Nope."

"Fine." Dr. Shook leaned forward. "Would you mind all that much giving me permission to search your locker?"

"If I *did* mind . . ." Jackson said.

Dr. Shook's smile faded and his eyes narrowed slightly. "I'd probably see that as a failure to engage in the kind of open dialogue and frank exchange that our honor code demands."

Jackson raised one eyebrow.

"I'd probably have to write you up. And report you to CDSS."

Jackson almost laughed. All that jazz about sharing and personal growth—and this is what it came down to: *Open your locker, kid, or I'm gonna mess up your whole life, throw you out of my school, and send you to Paso Robles.* Shook could have saved a lot of time if he'd just said it right off the bat.

Jackson stood. "So let's go," he said.

Then he walked into the hallway, his heart thrumming in his chest.

Eric peeked out the window of classroom 29, study hall. He made a point to take as few classes as he could get away with, sitting around in study hall the rest of the time reading science fiction or listening to tunes on his iPod.

Yes! There was Jackson, walking briskly down the hallway. And Dr. Shook was following about five feet behind him with a grim look on his face.

Beauty! *Busted!* Man, if only he could be there to see it go down!

"Hi, Jackson!" It was that kid Nathan, the one that had driven him home the other day.

"S'up," Jackson said.

"All right. You need a ride home today?"

Dr. Shook said, "Nathan, Cody and I are sort of in the middle of something. Aren't you supposed to be in class?"

Nathan held up a pink hall pass that said bathroom on it. "Later!"

"Let's go, Cody," Dr. Shook said.

Jackson felt tired and wrung out. This was really bad. He walked to his locker, spun the dial on the combination lock, then opened the door and stepped back so Dr. Shook could see inside. There was a stack of books in the bottom. His book bag hung on a metal hook. Leaning in the back corner was a rolled-up newspaper, about a foot long, an inch or so wide, with blue masking tape around it. You couldn't see what was inside. But if you already knew, it was pretty obvious. Jackson tried not to look at it.

Dr. Shook said, "Could I ask you to remove the contents of the locker and place them on the floor?"

Jackson could feel his heart beating. He had this weird sad feeling, like he'd had a nice thing here and now it was gone. He knew he shouldn't have brought the stupid thing, that it was totally against the rules. It was just that . . . well, no point thinking about it. He took the books out first and put them on the floor. Dr. Shook stood there with his arms folded, not saying anything.

Then Jackson took out the rolled-up newspaper, setting it carefully on the floor next to the books so that the thing inside wouldn't fall out. His heart sped up a little more.

"The bag, too."

Jackson took out his black nylon book bag.

"Could I ask you to open it?"

Like he had a choice! Jackson unzipped the bag, held it up so Dr. Shook could see inside. Dr. Shook squinted, then took the bag from him, unzipped the side pockets. There was half a roll of Lifesavers in one pocket, an mp3 player that Elaine had given him in the other. Dr. Shook squeezed the pockets like he was making sure that there wasn't something inside them that he had missed. He set it on the floor next to the stack of books.

Dr. Shook stepped over the books and the rolled-up newspaper, looked inside the empty locker. His brow furrowed slightly, like he was surprised about something, then reached in and pressed on the walls of the locker—like he was expecting to find a secret panel or something.

Dr. Shook seemed puzzled. He stepped back, looked down at the books, picked one up, riffled through it. Then he set it back down.

"What's inside the newspaper, Cody?" Dr. Shook said. Not accusingly, but like he was just sort of curious.

Jackson didn't get it. Something was very odd here.

"Art project," Jackson said.

Dr. Shook stared at it for a moment, reached out as though to pick it up. But then stopped, stood up.

"Thank you very much, Cody," Dr. Shook said. He actually sounded kind of relieved. "I appreciate your patience. And your trust. See how easy things can be when you just trust and share and engage in dialogue?"

"Uh-huh," Jackson said.

"Go ahead and put your books back in the locker and then get back to class."

Dr. Shook walked away.

Man! Jackson felt drained. A flood of relief ran through him. Jackson watched the headmaster walk back down the hallway. That was *so* close. That was totally off the hook!

Jackson leaned over, picked up the rolled-up newspaper, and put it back in the locker. And that was when it struck him. Who had written that note? And if Shook wasn't looking for the thing that was wrapped up in the newspaper . . . then what in the world *was* he looking for?

After school, Nathan was walking out with Taylor when he spotted Jackson. "Hey, Jackson," he said. "Looked like something intense going on with Dr. Shook, huh?"

Jackson said, "Not really."

"No?" He sort of waited, expecting Jackson to

explain what had been going on at the locker. But when he didn't, Nathan just said, "Okay. So, you need a ride?"

Jackson shrugged. "Sure, okay."

They walked over to his car. Taylor got in the front seat. Jackson climbed in back. Ignoring Jackson, Taylor started talking about where she'd gone shopping the previous day.

Nathan started the car and pulled out of the lot onto the street.

"Hey," Nathan said, when Taylor finally stopped talking about dresses. "Got a problem. You know Eric McGorrill? He said I need to have a story if I want to win the election."

"Huh?" Taylor said. "Like a book?"

"No, like a narrative, a here's-who-Nathan-is kind of thing."

"Losing me!" she said.

"No, listen, it makes sense. Like, a story about how I need to get elected so I can get into Harvard so I can cure cancer."

Taylor looked at him, wide-eyed. "You're gonna cure *cancer*?"

Nathan sometimes wondered about Taylor. "Uh . . . no. That's just an example. I need a story that will make people want to vote for me."

"I get it." Taylor's brow furrowed and she held up one finger. "Wait. Wait. I know! You could tell everybody that you need to get into Harvard Law School so you can come back and take over as District Attorney of Los Angeles."

"Well . . . since my dad's already the district attorney . . . don't you think that would make me kind of look, like, unoriginal? Plus, you have to go to college before you can get into law school."

"Really? I did not know that." She chewed loudly on her gum as Nathan started driving toward Jackson's house. "Hey, I know. What if you want to be a famous fashion designer? And, um, being president of the class would help you . . . uh . . . uh . . ."

"*Fashion* designer?" Nathan said.

"Okay, fine," Taylor said. "You obviously don't need my help."

Nobody spoke until they rolled up in the neighborhood where Jackson lived.

"Which way?" Nathan said.

Jackson pointed to the right. They turned and Jackson said, "Here."

Nathan pulled up in front of a very small house with a neat yard and bars over the windows.

As he got out of the car, Jackson said, "The hero is never the biggest guy in the room. You need to be the little guy." He slammed the door and walked toward the house.

"What did he mean by that?" Nathan said.

Taylor popped her bubble gum. "What a tacky little house," she said.

Nathan drove off. *The little guy. The little guy. Hmm.*

SEVENTEEN

"I don't know what I'm going to do, Lex!" Daley said. "It was almost two thousand dollars!"

Lex was reading a book about chemistry. Without looking up, he said, "Offer a reward. A hundred bucks."

"Well, if somebody stole two thousand dollars, why would they exchange it for a hundred?"

Lex wrinkled his nose, looking at the page. "Did you know that if you mix saltpeter and sulphur and charcoal—"

Daley threw her hands up. "Not interested right now." She walked into the other room. Her father and stepmother were sitting at the table having breakfast. She dreaded telling them about it. But she knew if they found out because, say, Dr. Shook called, they'd freak.

"Ummm, Dad? There's something I need to tell you . . ."

Nathan hurried into school with just a minute to spare. As usual, he was running late. *Why am I always late?* he wondered. He'd get started on time, and then there was always some last minute detail to take care of. And next thing he knew, he was late. The hallways were crowded with kids streaming in from the parking lot.

Nathan spotted Justin, Art, and a couple of other guys on the football team. They looked at him with peculiar smiles.

"Playing hardball, huh?" Justin said.

Nathan frowned. "What?" he said.

"I love it!" Art said. "I am definitely voting for a man who's not afraid to roll around in the gutter!" Everybody laughed.

"What are you guys talking about?" Nathan said.

Justin and Art looked at each other and smiled slyly. "I get it," Art said. "Plausible deniability."

Justin and Art high-fived each other.

Nathan shook his head. He was totally mystified. "I gotta get to class," he said, "so I can go over those problems one more time before the test in math."

Daley knew that Nathan was in Mrs. Lindstrom's

homeroom, so she walked in and stood there with her arms folded, waiting. The thing that she'd seen in the hallway was making her blood boil.

"Uh-oh!" somebody whispered. There was a brief moment of nervous laughter. Daley glared around the room. Then the class went perfectly silent, all the other kids watching Daley. The bell rang for everyone to report to their homeroom.

Mrs. Lindstrom looked up from her desk. "Daley, are you planning on going to your class this morning?"

"In a minute, Mrs. Lindstrom," Daley said.

"Let's not make a big fuss, dear," Mrs. Lindstrom said.

But just then Nathan walked in. He brushed past Daley and hurried to his seat.

"Just like that, huh?" Daley said. She could feel the heat rising in her face.

Nathan looked up at her and blinked.

She shook her head. "I mean, I had no idea you could stoop so low."

Nathan's brow furrowed irritably. "What are you *talking* about?" he said.

"Oh, at least be a man and own up to it!"

Everybody in the class was staring at them.

"I don't know what you're babbling about," Nathan said.

Daley was trembling with anger. She couldn't believe he was such a jerk. "Don't think you're going to get away with this," she said. "I'm going to the honor council."

Nathan looked around and shrugged. "Could somebody tell me what this maniac is talking about?"

Everybody laughed. The bell rang.

She pointed her finger at him. "This is not over!"

Nathan was in the middle of the test in math class when Dr. Shook's voice came over the intercom. "Mr. Carter, would you excuse Nathan McHugh to come to the office?"

"He's taking a test, Dr. Shook."

"He can finish it later," Dr. Shook said.

"Busted!" somebody said.

Nathan turned his test over on the desk, feeling apprehensive. The test was not going so fabulously. And now this. Dr. Shook didn't call people out of class in the middle of a test unless something was wrong. He started having random scary thoughts. What if his mom or dad had been in a car wreck or something? He swallowed and then rushed down the hallway.

When he reached the administration area, Mrs. Windsor said, "Go right in to Dr. Shook's office."

Nathan opened the door and walked tentatively into Dr. Shook's office. Dr. Shook was sitting behind the desk with his fingers laced together, a very serious look on his face. Daley was sitting across from him in a chair.

"Sit," Dr. Shook said, looking grim.

Nathan sat, his heart thrumming in his throat. He wasn't sure if he was relieved or not. If Daley was here, then at least it meant that Dr. Shook wasn't about to tell him his parents were dead or something.

"Well?" Dr. Shook said.

Nathan looked at Daley. She glared back at him. He turned back to Dr. Shook.

"I'd like to hear your side of the story, Nathan."

"I'm kind of lost here," Nathan said.

"Yeah, right," Daley said.

"Daley," Dr. Shook said, "let's try to keep this on a civil basis."

"Dr. Shook," Nathan said, "I walked into class this morning and Daley was standing there accusing me of something. But I still don't know what she's talking about."

Dr. Shook studied Nathan's face. "You're really going to make me spell this out?"

Nathan spread his hands feebly. "I guess."

Dr. Shook drummed his fingers on the desk for a minute. "All right, then. Follow me."

Nathan stood and followed Dr. Shook out of the office and into the hallway. Daley came behind him, muttering something that Nathan couldn't quite make out.

They walked around the corner and into the big hallway outside the cafeteria.

"Well?" Dr. Shook said for the second time.

"What?"

Dr. Shook waved his hand at the wall. The hallway outside the cafeteria was two stories high, with a very long, high wall stretching the entire length of the cafeteria entrance.

It took Nathan a second. But then he saw. He could feel the blood draining out of his face.

This was not good.

Daley stood with her arms crossed, watching Nathan's face as he looked up at the row of giant posters. Somebody had torn all her posters down. The floor was littered with ripped up shreds of cardboard. They had been replaced with Nathan's posters. One said: STOP DALEY'S CAMPAIGN OF LIES! Another read: EMPTY PROMISES. DALEY CAN'T DELIVER. Another one said: WHERE'S THE MONEY, DALEY?

And the worst, duplicated on at least six or seven other posters, showed Daley's face on a parody of an old-time "wanted" poster. This one had a grainy black-and-white picture in the center—a picture which had been taken from the eighth-grade yearbook. It was surely the worst photograph ever taken of her in her entire life. There was a big pimple on her forehead, her hair looked like a nest of birds, and her mouth was twisted into an awful tortured grimace as she attempted—unsuccessfully—to smile while hiding her braces.

Under the photo was one word:

UNWANTED!

"Wait a minute, wait a minute," Nathan said. "If you think I had anything to do with this . . ."

"Oh, give me a break!" Daley said.

"I *didn't*!"

"Of course you did."

"I did *not*!"

"Dr. Shook," Daley said in her most formal voice. "I want to bring Nathan in front of the honor council. This is a clear breach of the code of conduct."

"I'm inclined to think that's the right course of action," Dr. Shook said solemnly.

"Honor council!" Nathan said. "But I had nothing to do with this!"

Dr. Shook looked at him for a long time. "If that's your position, then we'll have an honor trial and you can make your case before the council."

"But . . ." Nathan spluttered. "But we're about to have an election. If she makes it look like I did this, then she'll win the election. This isn't fair!"

"Guys! Guys!" Dr. Shook held up his hands. "Settle down. The election is in two days. You know how this works, Nathan. According to the rules of the Hartwell honor code, if an accusation of an honor code violation is made, it automatically goes to the honor council. Unless Daley rescinds the accusation, we don't really have any choice in the matter."

Nathan looked at Daley.

"What?" she said hotly. "You're the only person who would have any reason to do this. I'm not rescinding anything!"

Dr. Shook shrugged. "Sorry, Nathan. That's it, then. The accusation stands." He looked thoughtful. "In fairness to your situation, Nathan, here's what I can do. We'll schedule the honor council trial for tomorrow. That way you'll get a chance to make your case before the election. The honor council isn't there to railroad you. It'll weigh the evidence fairly. If you are cleared by the honor council, then it shouldn't affect the election one way or the other. On the other hand, if the honor council finds that you violated the code . . ."

Dr. Shook didn't finish his sentence. He just walked over to the wall and began ripping down the posters one by one. When he had taken down all the posters, he turned around and said, "What are you waiting for? Go on back to class, both of you."

Then he marched off down the hallway toward his office, the offending posters rolled up under one arm.

"You probably put these up yourself, Daley," Nathan said, "just to make me look bad."

"You're beneath contempt, Nathan," Daley replied quietly.

Nathan looked at her for a moment, his brown eyes staring steadily at her. "Yeah? Well, everybody in the school's wondering. Where *did* that money go?" he said.

EIGHTEEN

Nathan came back to class and tried to finish the test, but he couldn't concentrate. The bell rang and he was still working.

"Nathan?" Mr. Carter said. "You need to hand it in now."

"But . . . I got called out by Dr. Shook," he said desperately. "Can't I get an extra ten minutes or something?"

Mr. Carter frowned. "Okay. Five."

Not that five minutes would make any difference. Nathan was getting killed on this test. Half the problems were still blank. All he could think about was the honor code trial. That was heavy-duty. The honor council had the power to make pretty much any punishment they wanted. They could even throw you out of Hartwell. It was composed of three faculty members and three students. If there was a tie vote, Dr. Shook came in as the tie-breaker.

Kids started filtering in for second period.

Finally Mr. Carter said, "Okay, Nathan, time's up."

Nathan scribbled a few more numbers and then handed the paper in. Mr. Carter looked at the paper and spotted all the blank spaces. "What's going on with you, Nathan?" he said. "Is there anything you need to talk about?"

Nathan shook his head and walked out.

As he came into the hallway, he saw Eric standing by his locker. Eric pointed his finger at Nathan and winked.

Suddenly it hit him: Had Eric put up those posters? He couldn't think of anybody else who would do something like that.

Eric turned away.

"Hey, hold on!" Nathan said.

Eric turned around and looked at him innocently. "Yeah?"

Nathan looked around to make sure nobody was listening. "Look, did you do it?"

Eric made a puzzled face. "Do what?"

"Come on, come on! The posters. Did you do those posters?"

"Me?" Eric put his hand on his chest. "Why would I do that?"

"Um, dirty tricks?" Nathan said. "Plausible deniability? Does any of this ring a bell?"

"Dude, I told you, I was just joking around. I wouldn't do something like that."

Nathan studied Eric's face. "This is no joke, Eric," he said. "I'm getting taken to honor council."

Eric's eyes widened. "Whoa! Bummer."

The tardy bell for second period rang.

"Seriously. Did you do this, Eric?"

Eric made a show of looking insulted now. "No! That's just not my kind of thing." Then he turned as though to walk away.

Nathan grabbed his arm. "Eric, man, you better not be messing with me."

Eric looked at Nathan's hand. "You want to let go of my arm? I'm trying to get to English."

"I could get thrown out of school. I could—"

Eric shook off Nathan's hand and started to walk away. Suddenly he stopped and whirled around. "Hey! This is it!"

"What?"

"Your story. Remember I said you needed a story?"

"Yeah?" Nathan said dubiously.

"Here it is! The man, falsely accused. Remember, like in that movie with Samuel L. Jackson? He's a hostage negotiator and he gets accused of doing something he didn't do? Great flick!"

"Didn't he end up having to, like, fight off the whole Chicago SWAT team and then burn down the whole building he was in?"

"Exactly!" Eric said. "Falsely accused! It's a total winner! Start telling the honeys." Then he walked away.

"Great," Nathan said.

When Eric reached the corner, he turned and called, "Of course, for it to work, the story has to have a big payoff."

"What do you mean?"

"You know, like the big dramatic moment in the honor code trial, the one where you reveal who *actually* did it."

"How am I gonna do that?" Nathan called.

But Eric was gone.

As Daley walked into class, she was still feeling wired from the confrontation with Nathan. It didn't really matter if Nathan got taken to the honor council. The damage was already done. Everybody had seen the posters. They might as well have said, DALEY TOOK THE MONEY.

She noticed Jackson sitting in the back row, staring at her.

"What!" she said.

"That money. You just left it there in a paper bag . . ." He sounded skeptical.

"I did *not* take the money!" she snapped.

"Did I say you took it?" Jackson said.

Daley suddenly felt puzzled. She thought back to when she realized the money was gone.

Jackson had been skulking by when she came out of the cafeteria.

"Wait a minute, Jackson," Daley said. "Did you see somebody steal it?"

Jackson looked like he was about to say something. But Mr. Hendershot interrupted.

"Class," Mr. Hendershot called. "Class, settle down and take your seats."

Daley sighed in frustration.

NINETEEN

RULE SIX:
TELL YOUR STORY
(ESPECIALLY TO HOT GIRLS)

At lunch, Nathan sidled up to Kerry Lynn Edwards, generally considered to be the second-prettiest girl in the school.

"Hi, Nathan," she said, somewhat nervously. Everybody knew about the honor council trial and they all seemed to be acting weird around him.

"So you heard about my trial, huh?" he said.

"Well . . ."

"Yeah, total raw deal," he said. "Everybody was looking at me all funny this morning and I couldn't figure out what it was. I didn't even know the posters were there until Dr. Shook showed them to me."

"They seemed a little mean," Kerry Lynn said.

"That's what you'd think," he said.

Her perfect brow furrowed. "What do you mean?"

"Well, I didn't put the posters up. So you have to ask yourself, *who did*?"

Her hazel eyes widened slightly. She put her hand on his arm. "Are you saying . . ."

"Hey, look, what if she's going for the sympathy vote? She tears up her own posters, then puts up these nasty ones, then I come off looking like some big jerk."

"You really think she'd do that?"

Nathan shrugged. "Hey, I'm just saying. Who stands to benefit if I get nailed by the honor council?"

"That just seems kind of twisted. I wouldn't have thought Daley was the type to do something like that."

He leaned toward her and lowered his voice. "Which is exactly what makes it so perfect."

Kerry Lynn stepped back slightly. "Taylor was looking for you."

Nathan looked over at the lunch table on the other side of the cafeteria where Taylor was sitting. "I better go see what's up with her." Then shook his head sadly and slapped himself in the middle of the chest. "I'm the victim here. That's what people need to understand. But I'm gonna reveal who really did it at the trial tomorrow."

"Wow!" Kerry Lynn said.

As he made his way toward the table where Taylor was sitting, Katie Chun stood up in front of him. She was co-captain of the cheerleading squad. "Hi, Katie," he said.

She looked at him for a moment. "I heard the

Shookster's going after you about those silly posters."

He leaned forward and said in a confidential tone, "You know, tomorrow in the trial? I'm gonna reveal the truth about that. Listen to this . . ."

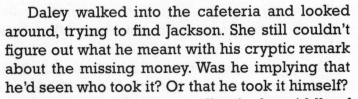

Daley walked into the cafeteria and looked around, trying to find Jackson. She still couldn't figure out what he meant with his cryptic remark about the missing money. Was he implying that he'd seen who took it? Or that he took it himself?

She noticed Nathan standing in the middle of the room, chewing on an energy bar and laughing about something while he talked to Katie Chun. He looked like he didn't have a care in the world. Suddenly Daley's eyes met his.

Nathan's smile died. He leaned closer to Katie and whispered something to her. She looked at Daley, too, then her eyes widened slightly at something Nathan said.

What kind of lies was he spreading? After the posters he'd put up, she wouldn't put anything past him.

Daley finally spotted Jackson out in the hallway. He was down at the far end of the hallway, the one leading to the Art Annex. He was carrying something in his hand, something rolled up in a piece of newspaper with blue tape wrapped around it.

"Hey!" she yelled. "Jackson."

But he stepped around the corner and was gone. She hurried down the hallway and through the double doors leading to the Art Annex. As she did so, she saw Jackson disappear furtively into the door of the sculpture room.

She ran down the concrete path and followed him through the door. When she entered the sculpture studio, she saw him standing at the far end of the room. He was holding something shiny in his hand.

As soon as he heard the noise, he whirled around, looking at her expressionlessly. As he did so, he hid the thing he was holding behind his back.

"What?" he said.

"Uh . . ." Daley was suddenly feeling very nervous.

He began walking swiftly toward her. "Look—" he said angrily.

"Sorry. Wrong room," she said.

Then she stepped quickly back out the door and headed for the main building. Her heart was beating fast.

He had gotten that thing hidden behind his back pretty quickly. But not quickly enough that she couldn't see what it was.

A knife.

A long, shiny, wicked-looking knife.

TWENTY

"What, like, I'm not good enough for you?" Taylor said sarcastically. "I'm sure!"

"Where is this coming from?" Nathan said. "I told you earlier, I have to get my story out. See, Eric said—"

"I think you need to get your priorities straight," Taylor said. They were in the parking lot after school. Taylor had found him talking to Abby Fujimoto, and now she was flipping out.

"Come on, Taylor," he said. "You don't understand. I've got to get in front of this honor council thing ... "

"No, *you* don't understand." She gave him a significant look. "You don't understand everything I do for you."

"I'm just a little worried about—"

"I'm telling you, I'm sick of hearing you whine about this honor council thing. Listen to me, Nathan. I've got it covered."

"Look, you can't fix this. If I don't figure out who put up those posters—"

"I said, *I've got it covered.*"

Nathan frowned. "What exactly are you saying?"

Her face suddenly went blank. "Not important," she said, waving her red fingernails in the air. "Anyway, we're getting off the subject."

"What subject is that?"

"Me, of course!" she said, suddenly flashing him her blinding smile.

"Oh. Silly me."

Taylor didn't seem to catch the sarcasm. Her smile faded. "It's just that I'm tired of being taken for granted while you go around flirting with all the cute girls in the school."

"I'm not flirting!"

Across the quadrangle Melissa waved to him. "Hi, Nathan!" she called, grinning.

"See!" Taylor said.

"Oh, come on, we've been friends since I was a kid," Nathan protested. "Why are you being like this, Taylor? You're perfect. You have nothing to be jealous about."

"Jealous?" she said, hotly. "Who's jealous?"

Melissa stepped off the curb next to Nathan. "Hi, Taylor!"

Taylor narrowed her eyes at Melissa, then hopped in her Lexus and gunned the engine. The wheels howled and the car sped away, throwing up gravel.

"What was that all about?" Melissa said.

Nathan thought about it for a minute. What did Taylor mean, that she had the honor trial "covered"? The last thing he needed was for her to start bugging Dr. Shook. That would probably only make things worse.

Jackson was kind of hoping that guy Nathan would offer him a ride home again today—riding the city bus was a pain—but then he didn't see him after school. So it was back on the bus again. It wasn't all that far, but the way the bus routes ran, it took forever to get home.

As he was walking toward the bus stop down the sweeping drive in front of the school, he heard a voice behind him. "Jackson. Hey, Jackson."

He turned and there was Daley. Just about the last person he wanted to see.

She ran up to him and said, "Wait up, I need to talk to you."

He kept walking. If he missed the 3:05 bus, he'd have to stand around at the bus stop for, like, half an hour waiting for the next one.

Daley ran up next to him.

"Look, Jackson," Daley said, "this morning

you said something about the money that I lost. Something about a bag. How did you know about the money being in a bag?"

Jackson had reached the bus stop. He could see his bus coming. It was about halfway down the block. He fished into his pocket for his bus pass. "I saw you stick it in the bag."

"Did you take it?"

Jackson gave her a look.

"I mean, I could probably offer a reward or something if you give it back, Jackson."

Jackson held up his hand toward the bus so the driver would be sure to stop. Sometimes they'd just zoom by you if you didn't make it totally obvious you were riding.

"I saw what you were carrying," she said. "You know Hartwell has a zero tolerance policy about weapons."

"I didn't take the money," he said.

"Then what happened to it?"

As it happened, Jackson had seen what happened to the money. And if this girl had been halfway nice to him? He'd have told her in a heartbeat. But instead she had to come on like he was some thief. So he really didn't feel like telling her what he knew. The bus rolled to a halt.

"What *happened* to it, Jackson?"

The doors came open with a hiss of compressed air and several people got off the bus. Jackson started to get on.

Daley grabbed his arm. "You want me to tell Dr.

Shook about the knife? I can, you know."

"Your word against mine," he said.

The bus driver looked down at him. "You getting on or not, kid?" he said.

Jackson shrugged off her hand, climbed onto the bus.

"Wait!" she called. "Jackson. I need that money! *We* need the money. Otherwise we'll never get to Palau."

He walked down the aisle and sat down. She had a point. He was really looking forward to going to Palau. That was going to be about the coolest thing he'd ever done. Problem was, just because he'd seen where the money went didn't mean it was there anymore. It was probably too late to do anything about it, anyway.

Well, maybe tomorrow he'd tell her what he knew. Or maybe not.

"How am I gonna beat this thing in the honor council tomorrow?" Nathan said to Melissa. "I mean, I have no idea who put those posters up."

"No idea at all?" Melissa said.

"Well, at first I thought it was Eric. For some reason he seems to have taken an interest in my campaign."

"*Eric?*" Melissa said. "Huh. I mean, I guess he's a nice guy and everything. But he seems kind of . . ."

"Yeah, I know," Nathan said. She probably

didn't want to say *untrustworthy*. Melissa never said anything bad about anybody. But that's what she was thinking. "But he swore to me that he didn't."

"Then who else might have done it?"

Nathan shook his head. "I'm totally stumped."

"I mean, they must have come in before school yesterday. Maybe somebody saw them."

"Yeah, but who's here that early? Dr. Shook? A couple of the teachers, maybe? If they'd seen it, they would have reported it already."

Kids were filtering out of the school, climbing into their cars, and heading home.

"What about Earl, the janitor?" Melissa said. "Maybe he saw them."

"Worth a shot," Nathan said. "Let's go find him."

They walked back through the empty, echoing hallways, coming out the back past the Art Annex, then walking down the path to the maintenance shed.

Earl was sitting on an upturned five-gallon paint bucket in the back of the shed, working on the engine of a big mower, his cowboy hat propped on his head. "How y'all doing?" he said.

"Hi, Earl," they both said.

Earl smiled, his craggy face wrinkling up. "Heard you had a little excitement today, son," he said to Nathan.

"Yeah, that's what I came by to talk to you about. I was wondering if you saw who put up those posters by the lunch room."

Earl shook his head. "No sir, sure didn't."

"Did you see anybody wandering around the halls before school started?"

"Not to speak of."

"I'm kinda desperate here," Nathan said. "I mean, I know it *seems* like I'm the only guy with any reason to put up those posters. But I didn't do it."

"What about the security tapes?" Earl said. "They got a closed circuit TV camera at the front door. If you looked at the tapes from yesterday morning, you might be able to see who came in early in the morning."

"Hey, thanks, Earl!" Nathan said. "That's a great idea!"

Melissa and Nathan walked back to the front office and found Mrs. Windsor sitting at her desk. Nathan explained about his honor council trial and then said, "Do you think I could look at the tape from the security camera? It might show somebody coming in with those posters."

Mrs. Windsor grimaced.

"What?" Melissa said.

"We're supposed to put in a new tape every day. But sometimes I forget."

"Oh no!" Nathan said. "So there's no tape for today?"

Mrs. Windsor shook her head. "I'm afraid not."

Nathan sighed loudly. "I'm dead," he said. "I'm totally dead."

"Wait a minute, wait a minute!" Melissa said. "I bet those posters were made on the printer back in the Art Annex. The same way I made the posters for you."

"So?"

"Well, you have to log onto the computer to use the printer. You have to put your student ID number in and everything. So all we have to do is go back through and see who logged in during the past couple of days and we can narrow it down."

"Genius!" Nathan said.

"Good luck," Mrs. Windsor called as they hurried off down the hallway.

Nathan felt a sudden rush of relief. This would fix it!

He and Melissa practically ran down the halls getting to the Art Annex. They burst out the door and into the room where the computers were.

Nathan's heart sank. Seated at the computer next to the big poster printer was Miss Edmunds, the computer programming teacher. And standing behind her was Dr. Shook.

Dr. Shook looked over his shoulder. "Well, well," he said. "What have we here?"

"Uh . . ." Nathan said.

"I had an idea," Melissa said brightly. "Whoever printed those mean posters had to log into the computer, right? So if we find out who logged in, we'll know who printed them."

"Funny you should mention it, but that's precisely why we're here, too."

Miss Edmunds fingers were tapping sharply on the keys. "Okay," she said. "There's a log file here in the Windows sub-folder that . . ."

"You can skip all that mumbo-jumbo," Dr. Shook said. "Just tell me what we've got."

"Well, let's see. Here's the log. Okay. This computer has been used by three students in the past two days. The first one is you, Melissa."

"Sure," Melissa said. "That was from when I printed up Nathan's posters."

"The ones I made him take down?" Dr. Shook said.

"No, of course not! The first ones."

"Okay," Miss Edmunds said. "The second name is Daley."

"Aha!" Nathan said. "What did I tell you? She put them up herself to make me look bad."

"No," Miss Edmunds said. "This is just one print job of a single page printed twenty-five times."

"So that's twenty-five versions of the same poster?" Dr. Shook said. "Whoever put up those posters by the cafeteria made six different posters."

"Right," Nathan said. "So it should show six print jobs of one page apiece."

Miss Edmunds fingers tapped away on the keys.

"Right you are," she said. "Here it is. Six print jobs, one page each."

"Excellent!" Nathan said. "Nailed!"

"Who is it? Who is it?" Melissa said excitedly.

Dr. Shook and Miss Edmunds turned and looked gravely at Nathan. Nathan didn't like the expressions in their eyes.

"What?" he said nervously.

Miss Edmunds turned to the computer, pointed one finger at the screen.

There, in a little box that said "User" at the top, was a name.

NATHAN McHUGH.

"But . . ." Nathan spluttered, his eyes widening. "That's impossible!"

"Print this out, Miss Edmunds," Dr. Shook said. "And you—" He pointed his finger at Nathan. "I'll see *you* tomorrow at ten o'clock sharp."

TWENTY-ONE

When Jackson got home, he told his foster mother that he was going out to the library. He expected her to give him a bunch of grief. But instead she just shrugged wearily. "Be back in time for supper," she said.

He nodded and walked down the street.

Pretty soon he had reached the parking lot where Big Jay was waiting in the car, the big tribal tattoo running down the side of his face.

"Let's roll," Big Jay said as he climbed inside. "We got a lot to do today."

Dan Rosenthal pulled his car into the parking lot of a strip mall near the kid's house. It was a seedy little row of stores that all looked like they were about to go out of business. All the signs were written in Vietnamese or Cambodian or something. Rosenthal had been a Department of Social Services case officer for ten years now, and he'd pretty much given up caring about the kids he was supposed to be responsible for. Most of them were ungrateful little snots. He did the required home inspections and interviews, he typed up the reports, and then he went home and watched TV. Never gave the little creeps a second thought.

But there was something about this kid, Cody Jackson, that had gotten under his skin. Was it that the kid was so sullen and never answered his questions, didn't seem to be scared of Rosenthal? Or was it envy?

Dan Rosenthal had never caught a break in his life. His brother was a famous surgeon, and his sister owned a very successful travel agency, and every time the family got together they'd make cracks about how he was this broke forty-year-old loser. But this kid? No, it seemed like no matter what he did, things always came up roses for Cody Jackson. Despite running with all those crazy Samoans and despite being surly and never doing what he was told, despite his crappy family situation, despite all that—the kid had been the number two or three student in his class at Chavez. And then here he gets hooked up with the mayor's little pet project, Operation Second

Chance, to take kids out of the 'hood and put them in these fancy schools. How come nobody ever did anything like that for Dan Rosenthal? It made him want to puke: This little thug would probably get into some Ivy League school, end up being this fat cat millionaire on Wall Street or something, laughing at all the little people.

And Dan Rosenthal, meanwhile, would still be living in a dump, driving a ten-year-old car that leaked a quart of oil a week, doing a job he hated.

It wasn't right! No, this kid needed to be taken down a peg.

And Dan Rosenthal was just the man to do it.

He watched as Cody Jackson walked across the parking lot, looked over his shoulder like he was making sure that his foster mother wasn't following him, and then climbed into a hopped-up car with a bright yellow paint job and fat tires. For a moment it was hard to make out the face of the driver. But then the guy turned, and Dan Rosenthal saw the massive tribal tattoo crawling down the side of this character's face.

Yes! he thought. *I'm in business!* If the guy driving that street rod wasn't gang-affiliated, Rosenthal would eat his hat.

The car swung out onto the road, then headed east. At the next intersection, he turned south.

East and south. Beautiful! The car was heading back toward the crappy neighborhood that Cody Jackson had come from. Back toward all the stuff

Dan Rosenthal had specifically instructed him to stay away from. He was heading toward Gang Central.

Rosenthal pulled out onto the road and followed the yellow car, ignoring several idiots who had to brake to let him in.

Dan Rosenthal smiled. He was gonna nail this kid.

Rule Six. Tell your story. Tell as many people as you can. Especially cute girls. Everybody listens to cute girls, right? Even when they have nothing to say.

Everybody has a story that defines them, that tells the world who they really are, why they deserve to be rewarded in life. The only minor problem? I'm just not exactly sure what my story is. Well, I'll get it figured out.

And in the meantime, I've got an excuse to talk to a lot of honeys. How bad could that be?

Nathan finished recording his video, then sat down on his bed. What was he going to do? He had nothing. He thought for while, coming up with one strategy after another, each more desperate than the next.

Finally he opened the top drawer of his desk and fished around until he found a directory of all the kids at school. It had their phone numbers and everything. He ran his finger down the list, starting with the A's. Ellen Abercrombie. Didn't really know her. Jim Addison. Hm. Barely knew the guy. But it was worth a shot.

He took a deep breath, picked up the phone, and dialed the number. "Hey, Jim, buddy," he said. "It's Nathan . . . McHugh. Yeah, look, I got a question for you. By any chance did you see anybody who might have put up those posters? No? Okay, okay, yeah. Thanks, bro."

Rosenthal parked on the street about a block down from the place where the yellow car that he was following had pulled in. He waited for a minute to see if it would drive out again. It didn't. So he turned off the air conditioning, climbed out of the car, and walked down the street.

It was an industrial area in one of the sketchier neighborhoods on the fringes of central LA. There were gang tags painted everywhere. Definitely the kind of area where Jackson wasn't supposed to be hanging out.

Rosenthal spotted the yellow car parked behind a rusting chain link fence. There were a bunch of hopped-up foreign cars inside the fence. Behind them was a cinderblock building with the word YOMA painted on the wall. Yoma? What was that? Some kind of Samoan word? The rest of the building had all kinds of weird Samoan art painted on it. The place looked like a gang hangout. There were several large bay doors in the wall of the building, with cars jacked up on lifts inside.

Maybe this was a chop shop—a garage where they cut up stolen cars and sold them for parts. Yeah, ten to one, if he ran the plates on these cars through the crime computer, half of them would come up stolen.

Out front a couple of kids were standing around drinking Cokes. They had enough tattoos between them to open a circus sideshow.

Rosenthal brushed past them, walked through the bay door into the garage area. There were neatly stacked tool racks inside, everything clean and well kept.

Rosenthal looked around and spotted a pair of black sneakers sticking out from underneath a car. He leaned over a little and saw that it was Cody Jackson. He was probably under there stripping out parts to sell on the black market.

Rosenthal walked over, grabbed Jackson's ankle, and yanked him out from underneath the car.

It took a second for the kid to recognize Rosenthal. Jackson didn't speak, though.

Rosenthal took a guess: "I believe you told your foster mother that you were going to the library."

Jackson just kept staring up at him.

Dan Rosenthal smiled. "Busted."

Rosenthal heard a door bang behind him. A huge Samoan guy with biceps the size of footballs and a tattoo down the side of his face was walking briskly toward him. It was the guy who'd driven the yellow car. His eyes were hidden behind sunglasses.

"Something I can help you with, sir?" the big man said.

"I'm talking to the kid," Rosenthal said.

"Yes, sir," the big man said. "And I'm talking to you, sir. What are you doing here?"

Rosenthal reached inside his shirt, pulled out his badge. "I'm Cody's CDSS caseworker. This is between me and him."

"Not when you're on my property, sir," the big man said. His voice had a slightly threatening tone.

"Your property? So if I was to call in to the Department of Motor Vehicles, have them run all these vehicles through the computer, you'd be the one responsible if they came up stolen?"

The man stared at him from behind the dark sunglasses. He smiled slightly. "My friend," the big man said, "I believe you got the wrong idea here."

"Oh?" Dan Rosenthal said, smiling in a way that he hoped would cover up just exactly how nervous he was. "You're gonna stand here with all those tattoos and try to tell me you got no gang affiliation?"

"I *was* in a gang once," the huge man said. "But

that was a long time ago. Anyway, these tattoos are symbols of my heritage."

"Yeah, right," Rosenthal said sarcastically. "And I suppose this hasn't been a chop shop for a long time?"

The man laughed loudly. "Come here, sir," he said. Then he walked out the big bay door and into the parking lot.

Rosenthal followed him. "Okay," he said. "And?"

The man pointed at the sign above the door. "Y.O.M.A. You know what that stands for?"

Rosenthal hadn't noticed the periods from the road. "Not really."

"Youth Outreach Ministries Associated," the big man said. "From the outside, this place looks like a garage. But it's not."

Rosenthal blinked. "Huh?"

"Basically, this place is—"

"What, a gang hideout?"

The huge guy stared at him for about a minute. "No, sir," he said finally. "It's a church."

"Oh, please!"

"Look, I used to be a banger. I know what it's like. Young boys, kids that live around here, the gang life's pulling at 'em all the time. But they all love cars. So I let kids come in, mess around with cars, soup 'em up, paint 'em, modify 'em. And while they're doing that, while I'm training them to be mechanics, giving them some job skills, I also start training their souls."

"A *church*?" Dan Rosenthal said.

"Jackson's probably the most talented mechanic I've ever trained. He's been coming here for three years now. He's still a little weak in the religion department, but, man, he can do things with an engine that you wouldn't believe."

"A church? He's been sneaking out of his house every day to come to a *church*?" Dan Rosenthal couldn't believe it. He walked back into the garage. Jackson was still lying on the mechanic's sled. "Cody, what's wrong with you? Why'd you lie to me and to Elaine about going to the library? All you had to do was say, 'Hey, I'm going to church,' or 'Hey, I've got a job fixing cars.' You could have saved me a heck of a lot of trouble."

The kid looked up at him with an expression that said: *Why would I want to do that?*

After his caseworker left, Jackson came out from under the car he was working on. Big Jay was standing there looking at him, arms crossed.

"What you trying to do, Jackson?" Big Jay said.

"What do you mean?"

"That guy's your DSS caseworker. He finds an excuse, he can make your life miserable."

Jackson shrugged. The truth was, he just didn't like this Mr. Rosenthal guy. Plus, he felt like there was stuff that was personal, that wasn't anybody else's business.

"All I'm saying, Jackson, is it wouldn't hurt you to be polite now and then."

Jackson didn't really have anything to say.

"I need to run down to the parts store, pick up a blower for that Civic over there," Big Jay said, pointing out the back door of the garage. "Can you keep an eye on things?"

"Sure."

Big Jay moved a little closer. "Look, some of your old running buddies came around here the other day looking for you. Couple of them are nice kids. But a couple of them aren't."

Jackson nodded. He had a hunch he knew what was coming next.

"Nothing personal," Big Jay said, "but I don't want those guys around here. They show up when I'm not here, you tell them to clear out."

Jackson hoped they wouldn't come around. It would be a drag having to tell his friends they weren't wanted around here. "Okay."

Big Jay studied his face for a minute and then said, "All right then. See you in a few."

Jackson got back underneath the car and started working. He heard the distinctive sound of Big Jay's turbo-charged engine start up and then drive off down the street.

For a while Jackson concentrated on the fuel pump he was working on. As usual, the mounting bracket holes didn't quite line up with the holes on the pump, so he was having to file out the holes with a chainsaw file to get everything to work. It was tedious, irritating work.

He had finally gotten the thing mounted and was about to hook up the fuel hose when he heard some noise coming from out front. Loud music. A song he recognized, the words all in Samoan . . . his heart sank. Crap, it was bound to be some of his old friends from Chavez.

He pulled himself out from under the car. For some reason, he hesitated. He picked up the knife he'd been making on the grinder and slipped the crude blade in his back pocket. Then he walked out front. Jackson noticed that Big Jay had closed the gate. There, just outside the gate, was a tricked out vintage Camero that belonged to his buddy Elvis. There were six kids crammed in the car. One of them was a guy named Moe, an older boy that Elvis and some of his friends used to hang out with. Moe was bad news.

A couple of heavily tattooed kids standing out front eyed Jackson as he walked out of the garage bay. "Y'all get inside," Jackson said. "I'll handle this."

The two boys didn't take any prompting. They disappeared. Jackson approached the fence.

"Whaddup!" Elvis called from the front seat. He looked friendly, but there was a note of challenge in his voice.

Jackson opened the gate just wide enough to slip through, closed it again behind him.

"S'up?" Jackson said.

The older guy, Moe, was looking at him from behind dark sunglasses, face impassive.

"Hey, bro, you gonna let us in?" Elvis said.

"Big Jay said we're not supposed to let anybody in when he's gone."

Elvis looked at Moe. "Big Jay?" Elvis said. He gunned the engine loudly. "You gonna listen to some half-baked preacher?"

"Hey," Jackson said sharply. "Come on . . ."

Suddenly all the guys were piling out of the car. "I mean, bro!" Elvis said. "We're still your friends, right?"

One of the other kids chimed in, "Or is that hoity-toity school getting your head all turned around?"

Jackson started walking, trying to get the guys away from the gate. "Gimme a break," he said. "You guys know me better than that."

"Okay, cool," Elvis said. "Then why don't you come roll with us?"

"I gotta finish up this thing," Jackson said vaguely.

Elvis looked at Moe. "He's gotta finish this thing," Elvis said. Elvis was smiling but he didn't sound friendly. He turned back to Jackson. "How 'bout next week? We were thinking maybe take a major road trip when school gets out."

Jackson shook his head. "Can't."

"Oh! You *can't*! Why not?"

"I'm going someplace."

All the guys looked at each other skeptically, like he was feeding them a line.

"No, seriously. I'm going on a school field trip ... to this Pacific island ... Palau." In his desperation to defuse all the tension, Jackson had been thinking that maybe—given that all these guys were Pacific Islanders themselves—they might think it was a kind of cool thing, a reasonable excuse. But as soon as it came out of his mouth, he knew he'd made a mistake. It would seem to them a betrayal, like he was jetting off on some kind of lavish beach vacation with his new rich friends. *Stupid, stupid!*

"Oh, a field trip!" Elvis said.

"With your *special* new friends!" another chimed in.

"Isn't that *marvelous*!" a third said.

Man. Jackson's heart sank. This was really bad.

Moe was leaned up against the door of Elvis's car. He hadn't moved an inch. He just stared at Jackson.

One of the kids, a big strong guy named BC who was always trying to impress Moe, poked Jackson in the shoulder with one finger. "Bro, you gettin' weak. Feel how weak he is."

Jackson took two steps back. He had his back against the rusting chain link fence now. He could feel the blade of his knife digging into his leg. He pulled it out, tossed it in the air casually, and caught it. Not trying to look threatening. But they knew what he was getting at.

"What y'all tripping about?" Jackson said, forcing a smile. He hoped maybe the knife would persuade everybody to back off, calm down. "Let's go down the street, get something to eat. I'm starving."

But the semi-circle around him didn't part. Everybody was looking at him, hard-faced.

"Elvis," he said, still tossing the knife in the air. "Why y'all stressing? You *know* me."

BC's hand shot out, banging Jackson's arm. The knife flew out of Jackson's hand and hit the ground with a clank.

Jackson felt a surge of fear. This was about to get really bad.

Then a loud voice spoke. "That's enough."

Jackson turned his head. Thank goodness! Relief drained through him. It was Big Jay. He was sure these guys wouldn't mess with Big Jay.

But he was wrong.

For the first time, Moe moved. "Nah, bro. *I* say when it's enough."

Big Jay turned and gave Moe a hard look. Moe looked completely un-intimidated. "You ain't nothing no more, Jay," he said. Then, suddenly, he shot forward, slamming into Big Jay. Moe was a big, strong guy. But he was no match for Big Jay. There were a couple of loud grunts and then Moe was on the ground.

In horror Jackson noticed that his fallen knife lay just inches from Moe's right hand. He tried to jump forward and grab it before Moe could get to it. But BC slammed Jackson back into the fence. Moe's fingers closed around the knife, then he rose to a crouch. Big Jay whipped a stained oil rag from his back pocket and wrapped it around his hand to protect him from the onslaught. But it was too late. The knife sliced into his chest.

"You cut him, man!" Elvis yelled.

Even Moe looked shocked at the size of the gash in Big Jay's chest. It ran from one shoulder all the way down to the other side of his belly.

At the same moment Jackson saw a police car come careening around the corner, lights flashing. Somebody must have called 911.

"Five-oh!" one of the kids yelled. "Five-oh!"

Big Jay, bleeding from the massive gash across his chest, jumped forward and slammed Moe in the face. Moe went down to the ground, the knife spinning out of his hand. He began crawling toward the car. "Let's roll!" he hissed.

BC took the opportunity to slam his elbow into Jackson's stomach. Jackson fell to the pavement, gasping.

The boys ran to the car, piled in, slammed the doors. The huge V8 roared and the Camero leapt forward.

Big Jay staggered into the street, chasing after them. Blood poured from his shirt now, dripping onto the ground. Jackson got slowly to his feet, trying to catch his breath. The police car grew closer and closer.

Big Jay's knees buckled as the police car slammed to a halt. Then he fell to the ground.

Two policemen jumped from the car, guns drawn.

"Ambulance!" the driver yelled into his shoulder microphone. "We need an ambulance!"

Big Jay was holding his chest. He pointed toward the knife. Jackson realized what he was getting at. It was his knife. If the cops found out who it belonged to, Jackson would be in big trouble. Even if he hadn't done anything. He knew he had to get the knife out of there.

He met Big Jay's eyes. "Go," Big Jay whispered.

Then he lost consciousness and pitched forward onto his face.

Jackson scooped the knife off the ground, slid through the gate into the parking lot, and began to run.

TWENTY-TWO

Lex was sitting in the living room doing a book of puzzles when Daley got home. She didn't say anything to him, just walked up and down in the living room muttering to herself. After a while she flung herself down on the couch. Her hands were trembling.

"Why do I do this?" she said. "Why? Why do I let him get under my skin like this?"

"I don't know," Lex said. "You tell me." He had no idea what she was talking about. But that was Daley. Always getting worked up about something.

She put her hands over her face, then her shoulders started shaking.

"Agh!" she shouted.

Then she rushed out of the room and went into the hallway bathroom.

Lex was always getting lectures from his mom about giving Daley her personal space and all this junk. But he was kind of wondering what was wrong.

What could he do? He was curious. That was just the way he was.

He went over to where she had tossed her backpack, reaching into it and pulling out a crumpled sheet of poster paper. He unballed the paper, and smoothed it out. It said,

STOP DALEY'S CAMPAIGN OF LIES!

Probably something to do with her stupid election. Boy, she sure did get upset over piddly stuff. This was obviously just a joke. Lex was about to ball it up again and throw it away. But then he noticed something interesting.

He took out a pen and paper and copied something down off the poster. *Hmm. Let's see now . . .*

At dinner that night, Nathan told his family about the honor code trial. He told them that he had called probably half the people in his class asking if anybody knew about the posters. And no one knew anything.

"So I need your advice, Dad," Nathan concluded. "You're a lawyer. What do you think I should do at the honor trial tomorrow?"

Nathan's father looked thoughtfully up in the

air for a moment. "About this computer . . . any way that somebody else could have logged in as you?"

"Well, obviously somebody did. Anybody could do it if they knew my ID number."

"Who knows your number?"

"It's not like it's some big secret," Nathan said. "You have to use it any time you're on the computer. And when you buy lunch. And for lots of other stuff. So anybody could just look over your shoulder when you're punching it in and find it out."

"Anybody specifically you've given it to?"

Nathan shook his head. "Well . . . maybe Melissa."

Nathan's father frowned. "I assume you don't think—"

"No way!"

"Okay then," his father said. "If this were a criminal trial, I would say that you could still raise the possibility that she did it and develop reasonable doubt. But this is not that kind of trial. This is about your honor. And you couldn't honorably blame it on your friend."

Nathan shook his head. "No."

"Well, let's face it, son, your pass code wasn't chosen randomly by whoever did this. They obviously expected that Dr. Shook would discover the pass code. In other words, they framed you."

Nathan nodded, waited for his father to say something else.

But his dad just looked at him silently.

"Come on, Dad! You gotta give me something here."

Nathan's father looked uncomfortable. "Are you familiar with the concept of a plea bargain?"

"Um . . ."

"Every year we handle thousands and thousands of cases. We don't have time to try them all. So if people come to us and say, 'Okay, I admit I did it,' sometimes we'll reduce their sentence a little bit. Basically just to get rid of the case."

Nathan's eyes widened. "Are you saying I should tell them that I did something that I didn't do?"

Nathan's father sighed. "If you genuinely didn't do this, then you should fight it. But recognize that you could lose. And it might be that they would be more lenient on you if you apologized and said you'd made a mistake than if you kept protesting your innocence right down the line."

"But that's crazy!"

"Sometimes the world is crazy, son."

Nathan felt like he was going to cry for a minute. "But I'll lose the election! And I'll look like I'm this total jerk."

Nathan's father cut a piece of chicken in half. "Unless you can find out who did it, you're probably going to lose your trial. But if you tell them you did it, when you didn't, well, that would be dishonorable."

"Then what . . ."

"My advice?" Nathan's father said. "Go in there and show them who you are. Stand up straight, look them in the eye, show them your dignity and your seriousness and your character. And then tell the truth. And just hope they believe you."

Suddenly Nathan didn't feel like eating very much. He pushed his plate away. He had been expecting some brilliant solution from his dad. But his father had given him nothing.

"It's going to be fine," his mother said. "*We* know you didn't do it."

"That's not good enough!" Nathan said, jumping up from the table.

He ran down the hallway, up the stairs, and into his bedroom. Then he flung himself on the bed and lay there face down.

This, he thought, *is the worst day of my life.*

TWENTY-THREE

The honor council met in an airy conference room that was generally only used by the board of directors of the school. In the center of the room was a conference table made from pale wood that seemed about as long as an aircraft carrier. The furniture was all very modern and cool-looking.

When Nathan entered the room, the council members were already seated. At the head of the table sat Dr. Shook. On one side of the table were the student representatives, all of them seniors, all of them looking serious and important. The teachers were on the other side of the table—Mrs. Eldon, Coach Lesley, and the scariest woman in the school, Mrs. Ng, the calculus teacher.

Nathan's stomach was feeling queasy and his head ached. He hadn't slept a wink that night and his mouth was dry. He felt slightly light-headed, the way you sometimes feel when you stand up too quickly and the blood rushes out of your head. He wished he could just run away.

Daley was already sitting near the end of the table.

Dr. Shook smiled. It wasn't exactly a phony smile, but he didn't quite seem to mean it, either. "Sit, Nathan," Dr. Shook said. "I know you know everybody here, so let me begin by familiarizing you with the procedure."

Nathan sat. The chair was extremely uncomfortable, the hard leather cutting into his legs. He shifted around but couldn't find a position that felt right.

"Now don't get all worried and nervous, Nathan!" Dr. Shook said cheerily. "This isn't the Spanish Inquisition here. We're all friends in this room."

Sure, Nathan thought. Daley's green eyes stared impassively at him. *With friends like that . . .*

"As you know, here at Hartwell, we're not about punishment and making people feel bad. We're about character. The honor code is cherished here because it's intended to encourage the highest standards of honor and character in our students. So . . . we want to accomplish two things in this room. First, we want to establish the facts. You've been accused of putting up posters accusing Daley Marin of being dishonest. We'll try to establish whether you, in fact, are responsible for putting up the posters.

"Second, we want to help achieve a resolution which will result in personal growth and healing for all parties involved. If, in fact, you put up these posters, the best thing you could do is to acknowledge that fact in a forthright and honest way. It would count a great deal toward whatever, ah, sanction we might choose to impose. Clear?"

"Yes, Dr. Shook," Nathan said. *Sanction.* That was a fancy word for punishment.

"This isn't a real formal event," Dr. Shook said in his heartiest tone of voice. "We call it a trial, but I like to think of it as more of a friendly discussion! We discuss the facts. We bring in any witnesses who might be involved and we chat with them. Then we discuss the implications of whatever factual matters have been raised. I'll moderate, but everyone should feel free to jump right in with any questions or concerns." He flashed the half-hearted smile again. "How's that sound?"

"Fine," Nathan said. His voice sounded shaky.

"Terrific!" Dr. Shook clapped his hands together once, loudly.

"Before we get started," Nathan said, "what's the worst thing that could happen?"

"Oh, let's not get all bogged down in negatives," Dr. Shook said.

But Mrs. Ng leaned forward and said, "Come on, don't candy-coat it, Garland." She turned toward Nathan. She was a very small, beautiful woman with glittering black eyes that seemed to look right through you. "If you did it and you're not willing to confess, then we can throw you out of Hartwell and give you an incomplete for the year. If that happens, you'd probably have to repeat the entire grade in some other school. It will very likely ruin your chances of getting into a top college. I'm not saying we will. But we could."

Nathan swallowed. "So basically if I say I did it, then you'd go easier on me?"

Dr. Shook lifted one finger off the table and gave a tiny shrug. Which was his way of saying yes. It was turning out just like Nathan's dad had said.

Nathan looked at the faces around the table. He felt very small and alone. Daley looked at him expressionlessly. But it seemed like she was trying not to give him a big, smug smile. This was so bad. This was so totally bad.

Dr. Shook said, "Are you suggesting you have something to say before we get started?"

Nathan took a deep breath, and sat up straight. It was like his dad had said. Show your character and hope for the best.

He looked Daley in the eye for a moment, then met Dr. Shook's gaze. "The first time I saw the posters was when Dr. Shook showed them to me. I had nothing to do with them being put up. Daley and I have our differences. And I'd like to win this election. But I would never, ever accuse somebody of doing something that they didn't do."

He looked around the room and met everybody's eyes in turn. He had a hunch they didn't believe him even a little bit.

"All right, then," Dr. Shook said. "Let's move along. Daley, how about we begin with you."

Daley stood. "Two days ago, I was selling raffle tickets for the camping club fund-raiser. We had collected about nineteen hundred dollars just during lunch. At the end of second lunch period I put the money in a paper bag and left it with Jory Twist. She didn't realize I had left the money with her, so when Dr. Shook told her to go to class, she left, not knowing the money was lying there on the floor. When I came back, the money was gone.

"The next day I came into school and I saw that all my posters outside the lunch room had been torn down and left on the floor. Six posters had been put in their places."

"Could you show them to us?" Dr. Shook said.

Mrs. Windsor looked up at the visitor who had just entered the front door of the Hartwell School. He was a tall, distinguished-looking man in a suit that looked like it had cost more than Mrs. Windsor's car.

"Yes?" she said.

"Good morning." The distinguished man smiled easily and set a cream-colored business card on the countertop. "Michael O'Keefe, attorney-at-law. I'm here to see Miss Taylor Hagan."

Mrs. Windsor frowned. "And what's this in reference to?"

"Miss Hagan is my client."

Mrs. Windsor was confused. "This is a school, sir. Only parents are allowed to see children during school hours. If you need to conduct business with her—"

The lawyer interrupted, "Yes, yes, naturally. I've been retained by Miss Hagan's father while Mr. Hagan is in Switzerland on business. I am authorized to act *in loco parentis*. That means that under California state law, I am effectively her parent. Here's all the documentation." He set a very shiny leather briefcase on the counter, pulled out a pile of paper, and slid it across the countertop. There was a bunch of legal mumbo-jumbo printed on it that didn't really mean anything to Mrs. Windsor. "Power of attorney. Directive of parental responsibility. Et cetera, et cetera. I'm afraid by law you must grant me access to the young lady right now." He smiled broadly. "Unless, of course, you'd like to be charged with kidnapping."

She cleared her throat. "Sir? Let me go get Dr. Shook."

"Superb!" the lawyer said, slapping one hand down on the counter. "I'll wait right here."

"Go on, Daley," Dr. Shook said.

Daley felt a flutter of nervousness. Not bad nervousness, just a hint, like the minute before she'd started the debate club finals earlier this year at UCLA.

Daley picked up some posters from the floor and held them up in sequence. She started with the one that said STOP DALEY'S CAMPAIGN OF LIES and continued slowly through all the posters. She had carefully ordered them for maximum shock value.

Finally Daley got to the one that looked like a "wanted" poster, the one with her terrible eighth-grade yearbook photo that said WOULD YOU TRUST THIS FACE?

"Oh! Brutal!" Jim Berman, the president of the senior class, laughed loudly.

Mrs. Ng gave him a hard look and his laugh died in his throat.

"Uh," he said, "I mean, I'm just saying. It's pretty bad."

Jim was still obviously trying to stifle a smirk. Daley blinked. "So, Jim," she said. "You think it's funny?"

Jim Berman "Well . . ."

"Actually, I do, too," she said. "And that's why it's so bad. I mean, God, look at this picture. I look like some kind of freak. You know how embarrassed I was back in eighth grade when this picture showed up in the yearbook? And to drag it out now? I mean, this stuff is all really clever. Really funny. In a way, that's what makes it so mean and nasty and spiteful."

"Anything else to add?" Dr. Shook said.

She took out the notes she had printed on her

computer the night before. They ran to five pages. Single-spaced. "Actually," she said with a tight smile, "I'm just getting started."

She looked down at Nathan. He was looking at the tabletop. His face was pale and he looked scared witless. Served him right!

The door opened and Mrs. Windsor poked her head into the room. "Dr. Shook? Could I bother you for just a second?"

"Doris, we're kind of in the middle of something."

"I really think you need to come out here."

Dr. Shook frowned. "Let's take a breather, guys," he said. "Relax, and I'll be right back."

———

"What's this all about?" Dr. Shook said as he came out to the counter. A silver-haired man in a custom-made suit was standing with his back turned. The man turned and smiled broadly.

"Hello, Garland!" he said pleasantly. "Michael O'Keefe from O'Keefe, Bain, and Ridge. I think we've met."

Dr. Shook recognized the man. He was one of the top lawyers in the city, the kind of guy who probably charged a thousand dollars an hour to his clients. "Mr. O'Keefe, yes, yes, sure," Dr. Shook said. He would have remembered meeting a guy like Michael O'Keefe—and he was quite sure he hadn't.

"No, no, my friends call me Mike." He reached out and clasped Dr. Shook's hand, nearly crushing it in his powerful grip.

"So, what can I do for you, uh, Mike?" Dr. Shook said.

"I just need a quick conversation with my client, Miss Taylor Hagan."

"Client?"

"Rex Hagan sent me over to straighten a few things out that really just can't wait. I trust you can spare a moment or two to chat with me after I talk to Miss Hagan?"

Taylor Hagan's father, Rex Hagan, had donated more money to the Hartwell School than anyone in recent memory. This whole thing was extremely puzzling. But you didn't step on the toes of a guy who gave one point three million dollars to the school last year. "Oh, sure, naturally, not a problem," Dr. Shook said. "Mrs. Windsor, would you call Taylor Hagan out from class? And grab a cup of coffee for Mr. O'Keefe, too, would you?"

"No, no, I'm fine," the lawyer said.

"I'm kind of in the middle of something," Dr. Shook said. "If you'll forgive me . . ."

The lawyer slapped him on the shoulder like they were old friends. "By all means, Garland. By all means."

Dr. Shook came back into the room and sat

down, an odd expression on his face. "Go ahead, Daley."

Daley cleared her throat. "Yes, I'd like to call my first witness."

"Witness?" Dr. Shook looked uncertainly at Mrs. Ng. Mrs. Ng nodded.

"Thank you," Daley said. "I'll be right back." She went outside. Mrs. Ralph, the art teacher, was sitting outside the door.

They both walked in. "Mrs. Ralph, I just have a couple of quick questions. Is Nathan in your art class?"

Mrs. Ralph looked at Nathan briefly. "Yes, he is."

"And does he know how to use the programs on the computer in the Art Annex?"

"Yes. In fact, he's probably the most proficient student in the class. He's a whiz with computers. So I've let him concentrate on graphics and video arts."

"So he can use the program that prints posters on the big printer in there."

"Sure. In fact, I've encouraged him to train other students in the software. Just last week he was helping Taylor Hagan. Her work improved dramatically after that."

"Thank you for taking time from your break, Mrs. Ralph," Daley said.

Mrs. Ralph left. "I just have one more witness," Daley said. She walked out the door again. Her brother Lex was sitting in a chair reading a book about bugs. "You're on," she said.

"Okay." He hopped up and walked into the conference room.

"I think you all know my brother, Lex," Daley said. "He's in Hartwell's elementary school program next door." She pointed at the elementary school building, which was visible out the window on the other side of the quadrangle.

"Hi," Lex said. He didn't seem at all intimidated. He held up his book. "I'm reading about stink bugs. They're really cool. They have very interesting antennae systems—"

"Thank you, Lex," Dr. Shook said. "That's interesting, but if you could—"

"I'll make it quick," Daley said, cutting off Dr. Shook. She turned to her brother. "The reason I've brought him here is because it seems to me that this case is all about how one person's actions affect other people's feelings. Lex, could you tell me about the day those posters were put up?"

"Oh, yeah, sorry." He didn't look sorry. "Here, hand me that poster."

Dr. Shook handed Lex the poster that he was pointing at. "See these little numbers down here?"

Dr. Shook and the other council members leaned forward and squinted at the corner of the poster.

"No," Dr. Shook said.

"Here." Lex pushed it closer.

"Oh. The little teeny-weeny numbers down here

in the corner. What is it, some kind of computer code?"

"Not really. See, I love puzzles that have to do with numbers. Codes and stuff like that. So anyway, Daley brought home this poster. I was, uh, kinda curious. So I pulled it out of her bag. The first thing I noticed were these little numbers. I immediately recognized that it was some kind of code. It's pretty stupid, really. If you look at it for a minute, you'll figure it out."

Everybody stared blankly at the corner of the poster.

"What, you don't see it?" Lex seemed genuinely puzzled that nobody had figured it out yet.

The headmaster shook his head.

"It's a baby code," Lex said. "1 equals A, 2 equals B, 3 equals C—like that."

"You want to save us the trouble and translate it, then?" Mrs. Ng said.

"It says, 'I am Nathan, king of the universe. I will crush Daley like a rotten mango.'"

"Let me see that!" Nathan said. He got up and walked over to the poster. Mrs. Ng was already scribbling a key on the edge of the poster, a little grid with A next to 1, B next to 2, and so on. She rapidly translated the message. Lex was right about what it said.

Nathan sat back down. "So, Lex, that's pretty interesting, what you found there. But does it prove that I did it?"

"No."

"So if somebody put these posters up trying to make me look bad . . ."

"You mean," Lex said, "like if someone was trying to frame you?"

Nathan looked at the council, then pointed to Daley's little brother. "He said it, not me."

Daley sighed loudly.

"Daley," Dr. Shook said, "we're having a civil discussion. No need for that."

Daley wanted to scream.

There was a tap at the door and then Mrs. Windsor stepped into the room. "I'm sorry to barge in again," she said, "but Mr. O'Keefe wants to speak with you, Dr. Shook."

"Sorry, guys," Dr. Shook said. "I'm afraid we'll need to take five again."

When Dr. Shook came back in, he was followed by two people. One was some old guy with white hair and a really nice suit. The other was Taylor.

Nathan looked at Taylor questioningly. She smiled back at him. It wasn't really a warm smile. What was she up to?

Dr. Shook had a strange expression on his face. "Well, folks," he said, "this is kind of an unprecedented situation. Um. You all know Taylor Hagan? This is her attorney, Michael O'Keefe. Apparently Taylor has something to say. I've spoken to Mr. O'Keefe here and, well, I'm not entirely happy with how this has worked out, but Mr. O'Keefe informs me that Taylor played, ah, some small part in this matter under investigation. And she's willing to tell us about it."

"Why the lawyer?" Mrs. Ng said.

"Mr. O'Keefe has kind of negotiated . . . uh . . . well, bottom line, whatever Taylor says, I've promised not to punish her for it."

"Oh, for Pete's sake, Garland!" Mrs. Ng said. "I'm not even sure that's allowed according to the honor council bylaws."

Dr. Shook looked at her nervously. "I'm not, either. But, guys, that's how it's going to work today."

What is this all about? Nathan wondered. This was totally weird. If Taylor knew something about this, why hadn't she told him?

Taylor sat down at the big table. Her lawyer sat next to her, between Nathan and Taylor, so that he blocked Nathan's view of Taylor's face.

"Taylor?" Dr. Shook said. "You have something to say that's pertinent to this hearing?"

Taylor leaned forward. "I'm not proud of it," she said. "But I did it."

The room was silent for a moment.

"Did what?" Daley said sharply.

"I printed the posters. I put them up." She shrugged and looked around her lawyer at Nathan. "Nathan didn't know anything about it."

Nathan felt his eyes widen. *Taylor?* Of all people,

Taylor was the last person he'd expect to do something like this.

"I think you need to explain this in a little more detail," Dr. Shook said.

Taylor looked down at the table. "Nathan's been having such a hard time in this campaign. And I felt bad because I wasn't doing anything. So I thought I'd surprise him and do something for him." She looked over at Daley. "I wasn't trying to be mean. Really. I was just trying to make a little joke."

"A joke!" Daley said. "You think it's a joke to accuse somebody of being a liar and a thief?"

"Yeah . . ." Taylor cocked her head slightly. "Bad idea, huh?"

Daley turned to Dr. Shook. "I think you just got sandbagged, Dr. Shook. Here she comes with her daddy's big lawyer to cut some kind of deal. Once she's got immunity, she can say anything."

"And?" Dr. Shook said coolly.

"Come on! How do we know Nathan wasn't in on this? She takes all the blame, the heat's off him, and he walks away scot-free."

"I just *said* Nathan didn't know," Taylor said hotly.

"Let's get real here," Daley said. "I don't like them, but I have to admit these are fairly clever posters. And—no offense, Taylor—but clever's not exactly your middle name."

"Um. Excuse me." A voice came from the corner

of the room. "Excuse me?" A small arm was poking up in the air.

"Not now, Lex," Daley said.

"Wait. Hold on," Lex said. "She said she made the posters. If that's true, why did she log onto the computer using Nathan's computer number?"

Everyone's heads swiveled toward Taylor.

"Good question," Dr. Shook said. "Why *did* you use Nathan's number?"

Taylor looked blankly at Dr. Shook. "Huh?" she said finally.

"See!" Daley said. "She has no idea what you're talking about. This is all a big fabrication."

"When we looked at the computer," Nathan said to Taylor, "my ID number had been logged in. Not yours."

Taylor frowned for a moment. Then her eyebrows went up. "You mean the little number that you type into the box at the beginning?" Taylor said.

"The little number you type into the box, yes," Dr. Shook said patiently.

"Oh . . ." Taylor blinked. There was a long silence. Nathan's heart sank. If anything, this was going to make things worse.

"Can we just get this over with?" Daley said. "It's obvious this is a desperate tactic to get Nathan off the hook."

"Wait! Wait!" Taylor said. "Nathan's the one who taught me how to use that program. Every time he showed me the program, he typed that number in at the beginning. I just thought that's how you did it."

"That little number was his ID number," Dr. Shook said.

"Well, how was I supposed to know that?" Taylor said.

"Maybe because all you had to do was read the little box," Daley said. "It says 'student ID number,' plain as day."

"Pshhh!" Taylor said. "Who *reads*, anyway?"

Daley shook her head. "This is so bogus!"

Taylor turned and looked at Daley solemnly. "Look, I just want to apologize. I really was just making a little joke. I promise I didn't mean anything by it."

Daley just looked at her.

"Daley," Dr. Shook said, "nobody saw Nathan putting up those posters. Nobody saw him working on them in the Art Annex. Nathan has been at Hartwell for ten years and he's been a consistently honorable and decent young man. I think that should count for something. I think we have to take what Taylor says at face value." He looked around the room. "I can't speak for the rest of the council, but I really don't see a need to take this to a vote."

Nobody said anything.

"People? Could we maybe have a motion that all charges against Nathan be dropped?"

"So moved," said Coach Lesley.

"All in favor?"

Everyone said, "Aye."

"Opposed?"

The room was silent. Dr. Shook smiled. "Since I

have agreed not to sanction Taylor for what she said, there's really nothing further we can do here. Daley, I think you should accept Taylor's apology and move on."

Daley looked like she'd just swallowed a bowl full of lemon juice. Finally she looked at Taylor and said, "Apology accepted."

Dr. Shook pushed back his chair. "Marvelous. I feel much better! I think we've had some real growth and progress happen here. Meeting adjourned."

TWENTY-FOUR

After it was over, Nathan approached Taylor in the hallway, his face flushed.

"How could you do that?" he said. He was trying to keep his voice low, but he was really peeved. She had nearly cost him the election.

"Do what?" Taylor said.

"Put up those posters! I mean, was that supposed to *help* me?"

Taylor blinked, looked at him angrily. "I was thinking maybe you'd thank me."

"For what?"

"For bailing you out."

"Well, if you hadn't put up the posters in the first place . . ."

Taylor rolled her eyes. "Get a *clue*, Nathan! You don't actually think I would sit around for, like, hours and hours printing out junk on a computer, do you?"

Nathan stared at her. A wave of astonishment ran through him. Suddenly he felt confused. "You mean . . . you just made all that stuff up? You lied to the honor council?"

"Well, why not?" Taylor said. "You didn't put up the posters, did you?"

"No, but that's not the point."

"Gosh, I'd sure like to know what the point *is*, then!" Taylor said. "If it hadn't been for me, all those goodie-goodies in the honor council would have thrown you out of school and ruined your whole life. For something you didn't even do!"

"I know, I know." Nathan stared morosely down the hallway. "It's just . . ."

"You can thank me when you go to Harvard and find the cure for cancer," she said.

"That's Daley, remember?" he said.

"What*ever*," she said.

As she walked away, Daley approached him and said sarcastically, "Well, congrats."

Nathan looked at her for a long time. "Do you really think I'd put up posters like that?"

Daley met his gaze for a long time, then finally said, "Well, I guess I *did* think so."

"Sure, I want to beat you," he said. "But fair and square. Not by cheating."

Daley's jaw was clamped shut.

"Look, we've got one more day till the election. Let's just try to do it right," he said. "Okay?"

"Okay."

"And, hey, I want to go to Palau as much as you do. Maybe if we work together we could find that money."

There was a hint of something in her eyes, a flash of vulnerability. "You think?"

"Worth a try."

"I guess you're right," she said, not meeting his eye.

"Bygones?" He put out his hand.

She shook it. "Bygones," she said.

"All right, then," Nathan said. "Let's find that money."

Dan Rosenthal was sitting in his crummy little cubicle at the Department of Social Services office when his phone rang.

"Rosenthal," he said.

"Yes, sir, this is Officer Shelnutt, LAPD. Are you the caseworker for a juvenile by the name of— hold on, let me look at my paperwork—by the name of Cody Jackson?"

"Matter of fact, I am," Rosenthal said. "Why?"

"Well, I'm just calling to give you a courtesy notification. He got picked up yesterday."

Rosenthal grabbed a pad of paper and a pen. "Where's he being held?"

"He's not. He was released."

"What was the charge?"

"What it was, we got a Code Six George on the radio. Initially it looked like a gang brawl type of thing. But once we took them downtown it got a little unclear. Looks like your kid was working at this ministry where kids learn to fix up cars. A couple of bangers had come down there and were hassling the kid. Then this preacher, a Samoan guy they call Big Jay, rolled up, tried to break things up, ended up getting cut. He's in a coma right now."

"So was Jackson charged or not?"

"Right now your kid Jackson is looking at a 243."

"Battery?"

"Like I say, I wouldn't be surprised if the DA drops the charges. There are several witnesses who say he was the victim here. And they never found the knife. Apparently your kid managed to ditch the blade before he got picked up."

"But right now . . ."

"Right now the charges still stand. And if this guy Big Jay dies, Jackson could theoretically go down for a 187."

"Murder? My, my, my. Well, thank you, Officer. I appreciate the heads-up."

Rosenthal put down the receiver and narrowed his eyes. This was going to take some thought.

Time to teach this little snot-nose some respect. He smiled and turned to his computer. This was going to be fun.

TWENTY-FIVE

RULE SEVEN:
THE TRUTH SHALL SET
YOU FREE (SORT OF)

So okay, I'm all about telling the truth. And the truth is, I didn't put up those posters. End of story, right?

Rule Seven. The truth shall set you free. Sort of.

I mean, do I feel bad that Taylor lied? Yeah, totally. But I guess the truth is never quite as clean as you'd like. Even though Taylor may not have really put up those posters, the truth is, I don't know who did. All I know is, it wasn't me. So what am I supposed to do? Go back to the honor council and say, "Well, I don't know who did those posters, but it wasn't Taylor, either"? No, that would just open up a whole new can of worms.

I just wish . . . well, whatever. I'll probably end up erasing this anyway.

Nathan and Daley sat next to each other at lunch, selling raffle tickets for the fund-raiser. They didn't speak to each other except to ask for change or more tickets. There weren't a lot of students buying raffle tickets, but the money continued to come in dribs and drabs.

At the end of second lunch, Daley counted the stack of bills. "One fifty-five," she said. "We got about two-twenty last period. It seems like the numbers are tapering off a little."

"So we've got, what, about three seventy-five—plus the missing amount," Nathan said. "So the total is just under twenty-three hundred."

"Assuming we find the missing money."

"So basically, at the rate we're going, if we get the missing money, we'll be going to Palau. And if not . . ."

"There goes the coolest summer of our lives."

They were silent for a minute.

"What do you think of this new guy, Jackson?" Daley said finally.

Nathan shrugged. "Seems like a nice enough guy. Sorta quiet."

"The reason I ask," Daley said, "is that yesterday he acted like he knew something about the money. But then—I don't know, maybe I made him mad or something—but anyway, he wouldn't talk."

"You?" Nathan raised one eyebrow. "Made

somebody mad? Hard to believe."

"Ha ha."

"I'll talk to him," Nathan said.

There was a moment of silence.

"He had a knife," she said.

"What do you mean?"

"A big, scary-looking knife. I saw him over in the Art Annex yesterday. He had a knife in his hand."

"Huh," Nathan said. "That's a little freaky."

As they were sitting there, the janitor, Earl, walked by with his big plastic bin on wheels, emptying the garbage cans.

"So you two worked it out, huh?" he said, pulling the plastic bag out of the trash.

"I guess," Nathan said.

Earl tied up the bag and tossed it in the big bin he'd been pushing. "See?" he said. "Good people will always find a way to work things out."

They watched him push his bin away and then Nathan said, "I'll talk to Jackson after school."

Eric heard about the results of the honor council trial at lunch. He was a little surprised by how things had turned out. As he was walking to class, he saw Nathan being accosted by several people.

"Heard about the honor trial thing, man!" one kid said. "Way to go!"

"Thanks! Have I got your vote?" Nathan responded.

"Absolutely!"

Nathan grinned broadly. It was obvious that he was immensely relieved now that the honor council thing wasn't hanging over his head. He seemed to have gotten his old confidence back.

Eric clapped him on the shoulder. "Big shocker, dude," he said. "So Taylor was the one who put up the posters, huh?"

Nathan's grin faded a little. "That's, uh, how it played out, yeah."

"Well, congratulations."

"Thanks." Nathan leaned toward him slightly. "I got your vote, right?"

Eric's eyebrows went up. "Dude! Is there any question?"

"You're the man," Nathan said.

"No, *you're* the man."

Eric rapped knuckles with Nathan, then stopped and watched him go. *Very strange development. Very strange.* Eric would never have expected Taylor to go in there and take the heat. She didn't seem like the kind of person who would do a thing like that.

As he was watching Nathan walk away, he felt something dig into his ribs. He turned around and there was Taylor Hagan looking at him, jabbing him with one of her long red fingernails. Eric's heart started beating rapidly and he felt a little sweaty. He got nervous just being near her.

"What's up, Taylor?" he said.

She looked at him with a funny expression in her eyes. "You tell me," she said.

"Huh?" he said.

"Just curious," she said. "How'd you get Nathan's ID number, Eric?"

Eric looked at her for a second and blinked. "Huh?" he said finally.

"Yeah," she said.

"I better get to class," Eric said. "Great talking to you, though. Let's do it again soon, huh?"

He walked away with this prickly feeling on his neck. *How did she know?* he thought. *How in the world did she know?*

TWENTY-SIX

RULE EIGHT:
TURN TRASH INTO TREASURE

Every campaign has some ups and downs, right? What are you going to do, freak out every time something bad comes along? No. When something negative happens, don't run away and hide from it. Take the negative and turn it into a positive. I got falsely accused? Fine. That's my story now.

Me? The nice guy, falsely accused. My opponent? A little vindictive, a little harsh. Who's gonna vote for somebody like that, right? Which leads me to . . .

Rule Eight: Turn trash into treasure. Take the negative, turn it around, ride it into the winner's circle!

After school, Nathan saw Taylor coming out of the building. He ran toward her.

"Hey," he said. "You're not still mad at me, are you?"

She held up her hand, put her palm near his face, and kept walking without looking at him.

"Hey, look, I really appreciate your helping me out with the honor council thing. I do. It just kind of took me by surprise."

She just kept walking. She was wearing sunglasses so he couldn't see her eyes.

"Taylor, come on, don't be like this!" Nathan said.

"Maybe tomorrow I won't be mad," she said, hopping into her Lexus. The window scrolled slowly down. She gave him a flirty little smile. "But then again, maybe I will."

She revved the engine and Nathan backed away.

As Taylor roared out of the parking lot, Nathan spotted Jackson walking out the door to the parking lot. He remembered his promise to talk to him.

"Need a ride?" he said.

Jackson shrugged. "That'd be all right."

They got into the car.

"No Beemer?" Jackson said.

Nathan laughed ruefully. "Not after you made me run it into the ditch. Dad said he'd never let me drive it again for the rest of my life."

He started the engine.

"Sorry," Jackson said.

"Hey, I can't blame you," Nathan said. "I'm the one who put it in the ditch." Nathan put the car in gear and headed down toward the street, but then said, "So look, you don't know what happened to that money, do you?"

Jackson looked over at him impassively. He seemed to be thinking about it. "I might," he said finally.

Nathan waited, but Jackson didn't say anything.

"Dude, if you know something . . ." Nathan said. "I mean, if we don't find that money, there's no trip to Palau."

Jackson sighed. "Turn the car around," he said.

Daley was standing at the pick-up ramp with Lex, waiting. As usual, her stepmom was late.

"You look bummed," Lex said.

Daley sighed. "I just feel weird. I kinda went out on a limb accusing Nathan of doing these posters, and now I'm thinking maybe he really didn't do it. I mean, Taylor, yeah, I could see her doing something that mean. But Nathan? I don't know."

"Did you apologize?"

"Hey, look, I saw him laughing at those posters. Well—smiling, anyway."

"So you didn't apologize."

Daley scowled. "All day everybody was congratulating him and slapping him on the back." She shook her head. "I'm gonna lose now. Everybody's gonna hate me. It's gonna be so humiliating."

A car pulled up in front of them. It wasn't her stepmother, though. It was Nathan, his elbow hanging out the open window of the car. And Jackson was sitting next to him in the passenger seat.

"Jackson thinks he knows something," Nathan said.

Jackson got out of the car. "Let's go," he said. Then he started walking into the building.

Nathan looked around nervously. You weren't supposed to park in the pick-up zone. But Jackson was already disappearing into the building.

"Come *on*," Daley said urgently to Nathan. "He likes *you*. Let's go."

Nathan shut off the car and hopped out. They followed Jackson into the building.

"Um," Lex said, "Mom's gonna be mad if we're not here."

"She's made us wait like a million times," Daley said. "I'm not gonna feel sorry about making her wait for once."

"Where we going?" Nathan said.

But Jackson just pointed and kept walking. Their footsteps echoed in the now-empty building. Daley felt a nervous sense of expectation. Did he actually know where it was? Or what?

They passed the administration offices and reached the hallway outside the cafeteria. Posters for both Nathan and Daley covered the walls.

Jackson walked past the folding table where they'd been selling raffle tickets and approached the trash can at the end of the hallway. He took off the lid and looked in.

Daley and Nathan crowded around the trash can and stared. There was a fresh bag in the can. Otherwise, the can was completely empty.

Jackson stared for a while. Finally he spoke:

"Oops."

TWENTY-SEVEN

Daley covered her face with her hands. "Oh no! Don't tell me!"

"That kid you were with," Jackson said.

"Jory?"

"Her, yeah. I saw her pick up this brown paper bag, throw it in the trash."

"Oh no! Oh no! Oh no!" Daley said.

"She must have thought it was her lunch bag," Nathan said.

"Why didn't you *say* something?" Daley said.

"All you had to do was ask," Jackson said. "Instead you accused me of stealing it."

"So it's been sitting there in the bottom of the trash all week?" Nathan said.

Jackson nodded.

"Well, it's gone now!" Daley said. "Congratulations, Jackson, thank you for screwing up our trip to Palau."

"Wait a minute, wait a minute," Nathan said. "Remember when we were selling tickets at lunch? Earl came by and emptied the garbage."

"So?"

"Hey, cool!" Lex said. "Dumpster diving!"

"Lex, could you be quiet?" Daley said. "We're trying to think here."

"He's right," Jackson said.

"If Earl just threw out the trash today," Lex added, "it'll probably still be out in the Dumpster behind the gym. Dumpster diving!" Lex repeated. "We're gonna go Dumpster diving! Cool!"

He started running toward the door that led out to the gym.

"Yippee," Daley said.

When they reached the back of the gym, Daley screamed. "Oh my God!"

"What?" Nathan said.

They came around the corner and there was a huge garbage truck parked in front of the Dumpster. The truck's engine growled loudly. Two large steel blades were slowly extending from the truck into the slots on the side of the Dumpster that were used to tip it up into the truck.

Daley ran frantically toward the truck, waving her arms. "Stop! Stop!" she yelled.

Everybody else followed.

"Stop! Stop! Stop!"

But the big steel blades continued to slide into the sides of the Dumpster. The truck emitted a loud grinding noise.

Daley waved her arms at the figure inside the truck, but he was paying attention to the Dumpster. He probably couldn't even hear them over the sound of the truck's motor.

The Dumpster shuddered, then rose slowly into the air.

Nathan ran up on the running board of the truck and rapped on the window. "Wait! Wait!" he yelled.

The Dumpster stopped moving. It was now suspended a good eight feet in the air.

The window came slowly down. An unshaven man wearing a stained baseball cap looked out the window. "Kid, you need to get off my truck," he said.

"Sir, I'm sorry to bother you," Nathan said, "but we need to get into that Dumpster."

"Yeah, right," the garbage collector said. He hit a lever and the Dumpster began to rise again.

"Wait! Wait!" Daley said. "He's not kidding. There's something really important in that trash."

The Dumpster stopped moving again. The garbage man looked down at Daley. "I don't really give a hoot what's in there. I got a scheduled collection. You need to get off my truck so I can get it done."

"Sir, hold on, hold on," Nathan said.

"This ain't a debate."

Before he could hit the lever, though, Jackson scrambled up onto the hood of the truck and climbed up on the Dumpster.

"Son of a—" The driver opened the door and hopped out. "Get offa there, kid! You're gonna get killed!"

Jackson didn't move, just stood there on top of the Dumpster, his arms crossed over his chest.

"Look, we just need a couple minutes to hunt through there," Nathan said.

Just then someone walked around the corner. It was Earl, wearing his big cowboy hat.

"What's going on here, folks?" he said.

"This idiot just got on my truck, Earl," the garbage man said.

"Howdy, Ray," Earl said to the garbage man. Then he turned to Jackson and said, "Not a great idea being up there, son."

"We think the missing money's in there," Nathan said. "Somebody threw it in a trash can by accident."

"Please, help us!" Daley said.

Earl had a wad of chewing tobacco in his mouth. He spit on the ground. "So, look, Ray, these kids lost them a serious bunch of money. You think you could drop that can, let 'em poke around in there a little?"

"Earl, I got a schedule to keep," the unshaven man said.

"I'd count it a personal a favor."

The garbage man rubbed his face thoughtfully. "I guess I could make a couple other pick-ups, run by here on the way back to the dump."

"Thank you, thank you!" Daley said.

The garbage man looked up irritably at Jackson. "Well, what you waiting for, kid? Get your tail off there so I can put the can down!"

Jackson leaped smoothly to the ground.

The garbage man climbed in his truck, lowered the Dumpster, and withdrew the big blades. As he was backing up, he poked his head out the window and said, "Listen up, kids. I'm gonna be back in half an hour. And when I get back, no fooling, I'm taking whatever's in that Dumpster."

They began searching frantically through the huge steel container. The problem was that there must have been close to fifty bags of trash in the Dumpster. Fifty stinking, leaking, smelly, gross, disgusting bags.

They worked furiously, flies buzzing around them as they ripped open bag after bag, sorting through the contents with broken broom handles provided by Earl, who watched from outside the Dumpster with a bemused expression on his face.

The more bags they tore up, the harder it was to find room inside the Dumpster to sort through each new bag.

"Can we throw them out on the ground?" Nathan called to Earl.

Earl shook his head. "Son, there's no way you'll get it all back in if you do that. Shook'll have my hide if there's a big old heap of garbage lying around here."

"Okay," Nathan said.

Daley was poking around in the latest garbage bag with a broom handle.

"Ow!" Nathan shouted, a sharp pain shooting into his foot. Daley had practically impaled him.

"Sorry," Daley said.

"No problem," Nathan said.

"Twenty minutes down," Lex called. "You've got ten left."

"Thank you for the math lessons," Daley said.

"How many more bags do we have?" Nathan said to Jackson.

He shook his head. "Can't tell. Ten? Fifteen?"

"Hurry! Hurry!" Daley said.

Jackson heaved another bag out and Nathan ripped it open. Old chicken bones and wilted lettuce and orange peels spilled out.

"I think I'm gonna gag," Daley said.

"Skip that bag," Jackson said.

"Yeah," Nathan said. "The one by the lunch room just has paper and drink cups and stuff."

They tore open several more.

"Five minutes," Lex called.

They had just ripped open the next bag when

they heard the sound of a diesel engine grinding up the road toward the Dumpster.

"He's early," Lex said.

"Hurry! Hurry!" Daley said.

Jackson fished out two more bags and tossed them over to Daley and Nathan. They tore them open. More spoiled lunch food.

They could hear the truck stop just feet from the Dumpster. The garbage man's voice came out of the truck: "Find it?"

"We're still looking," Nathan called.

"Well, hurry up!"

Jackson was hip-deep in garbage now. "Can't see," he said grimly. Nathan raked back some of the junk Jackson was standing in.

"Let's go!" the garbage man yelled.

"Got it," Jackson said, hauling out one last bag.

"That one's just paper, too," Daley said. "It's got to be it!"

She and Nathan tore it open. Inside were photocopies and drink cups and potato chip bags . . . but no brown paper bag full of money.

"Kids, I really gotta do this!" The voice of the garbage man.

"It has to be here!" Nathan said.

Daley and Nathan and Jackson all began frantically raking through garbage. But there was no brown paper bag.

Earl's face appeared above the lip of the

Dumpster. "Guys," he said. "You really need to let this fellow do his job."

Daley put her face in her hands.

Jackson nodded and began to climb out. Nathan and Daley followed.

They watched glumly as the Dumpster was lifted in the air and all the garbage spilled into the top of the truck.

"There goes two thousand bucks," Daley said.

"There goes Palau," Nathan said.

They turned and looked at Jackson. He looked at the ground.

"Well, sorry about that, kids," Earl said. "You sure somebody threw it away?"

Jackson nodded. "Yeah. In the trash can outside the lunch room."

Earl looked at Jackson. Then at Daley. Then at Nathan.

"What?" Nathan said.

"Saved yourself some aggravation if you'd told me," he said. "I think that one's still sitting in the bin up by the shed. Didn't get around to throwing it in the Dumpster."

Nathan and Daley exchanged glances.

"It's right up there." Earl pointed at the maintenance building.

Everyone broke into a run. The big plastic bin on wheels was sitting next to the door of the shed.

Daley looked in, broke into a grin.

"I'm not even getting my hopes up now," Nathan said.

"Well, I am!" she said, grabbing the big, black bag and heaving it out onto the ground. She tore open the bag.

The first thing to spill out was a wrinkled brown paper sack, covered with sticky cola.

She grabbed it, ripped it open. Five and ten and twenty dollar bills spilled out onto the ground.

"We're going to Palau!" Nathan shouted, picking up the money and throwing it in the air. "We're going to Palau!"

"Yes!" Daley shouted. She didn't think she'd ever felt so happy in her life. They'd done it! They were definitely going! And all this stuff about who stole it or who lost it or who could be trusted—it was all out the window now. She felt like a fifty-billion-ton weight had been lifted off her shoulders. She hugged Jackson, then Nathan, then turned toward Lex.

He held his nose and backed away from her. "Peeyewww! You stink!" Lex said. It was only then that she became fully aware of the fact that she was half covered in garbage.

"Don't even get *near* me!" Lex said.

She put her arms out like a zombie and began walking toward him. Lex began to run. Everyone dissolved into laughter.

TWENTY-EIGHT

RULE NINE:
MAKE A GREAT SPEECH

I'm lucky. My dad's this big-time lawyer. Like he says, "You spend twenty-five years in the court-room, after a while you learn something."

So I've been up all night working on my speech. And Dad's been helping. The first thing he said was to memorize your speech. Make it feel natural, not like some boring book report that you're reading off a page.

What else did he say? Relax. Have fun. Speak to everybody like you're having a conversation with a friend.

It's midnight right now and I've been going over it and over it for, like, six hours. But I think I'm ready.

Today was the big day! Election day.

Nathan jumped out of bed feeling a tingle of excitement and nervousness. And it wasn't until he'd walked through the front door of the Hartwell School that it occurred to him that today was the last day of school, too. He'd been so focused on the honor council trial and the contest with Daley that he had almost forgotten. Tomorrow they'd be on their way to Palau!

Wow. *Seriously* big day.

But first things first. He needed to win the election.

Nathan made a point to shake hands with every kid in every class he was in and to speak to everybody he saw in the hall. Most of the people he spoke to promised to vote for him. He felt like there had been a big change in momentum all of a sudden, like he was surfing on a wave of good feeling and confidence. For the first time since he'd seen Daley's glammed-up posters on the wall the day after they both announced they were running, Nathan felt like he was actually going to win.

People liked him! People trusted him! Hey, this wasn't rocket science. He was a nice guy and a trustworthy guy. They'd vote for him, right?

Daley had been working all night, too. She had

carefully outlined her twelve-point program with attention to the logic of every detail.

Then she had typed it up on her computer. It had run to six pages, single-spaced. That seemed a little long, so she'd cut it down. Then she'd felt like she was leaving out crucial points, so she beefed it up a little.

When she looked at the clock, it was four in the morning. And she still wasn't happy with the speech!

Her eyes felt like they were full of dirt. This was terrible! The speech was still way too long. She started cutting again. She felt overwhelmed by two contradictory feelings. On the one hand, she was exhausted. And on the other, she was scared witless of screwing up the speech. She sank into a fog, the white screen burning itself into her eyes.

Suddenly she was aware of an irritating beeping noise and something banging and banging. Then her stepmother's voice cut through the fog.

"Daley!" Gwen called. "Daley, wake up! You're already late for school! Your alarm's been ringing for an hour."

Daley sat up in her chair. "Oh my God!" she said. She hadn't overslept in years. And of all the days to choose, why this one? And of course her stepmother, who never paid attention to what time it was, hadn't even noticed.

The class assembly was at nine thirty. She looked at the clock. Eight forty-one. It took twenty-five minutes to get to school.

Oh God, oh God, oh God! This was a disaster. She wasn't even going to have time for a shower. At least she'd taken one the night before to get all the garbage stink off her skin.

She hopped out of the chair, heart racing wildly.

Nathan was standing on the stage, hands in his pockets, waiting for the assembly to begin. He was feeling strong, he was feeling confident, everything was coming together.

Where was Daley, though? Kinda odd. The bell had rang five minutes ago and kids were already filtering into the auditorium.

Dr. Shook took his place in a chair onstage and said, "Where's Daley?"

Nathan shrugged. "Beats me."

Dr. Shook frowned.

Nathan sat down and started going over the speech in his mind. The auditorium was full now, most of the kids seated.

Dr. Shook said, "We really need to get this started. Nathan, I was going to have you speak second, but if she doesn't get here . . ."

As his sentence trailed off, an agitated-looking Daley Marin rushed through the door at the back of the stage. "Sorry, sorry, sorry!" she said hurriedly.

Her hair was sticking up on one side of her

head, and she looked like she'd slept in the clothes she was wearing.

"If you need a minute to freshen up—" Dr. Shook said.

Daley cut him off. "No, no. I'm totally ready." She was pale and red-eyed, her jaw grimly set. You could practically smell the nervousness on her.

Nathan suppressed a smile. Why had he ever been worried? This was gonna be a cakewalk.

Daley was freaking. This was so bad. She'd been trying to go over the speech as her stepmother drove her and Lex to school, but reading in the car made her nauseated. So in addition to feeling woefully unprepared by the time she reached the school, she also felt like she was about to throw up.

She couldn't even concentrate on what Dr. Shook was saying as he introduced her. She kept concentrating on the first line. *Hello, everybody, my name is Daley Marin. Hello, everybody, my name is Daley Marin.*

Suddenly she was aware that the entire room was silent.

Dr. Shook was staring at her. He had already sat down and was gesturing at the empty podium.

"Daley?" he said. "Uh, Daley? Daley, you're on."

She jumped to her feet, rushed to the podium, feeling everyone staring at her. In her rush, she stumbled, only managing to catch herself by grabbing the podium at the last second. The microphone picked up the impact of her hand and a huge *whooomp!* noise thundered through the room.

A few people laughed. The laughter faded. Then silence. No applause, no nothing. She stood there, looking out at the audience. Everyone stared back impassively, looking like they'd rather be anywhere but there.

She fumbled with her notes. Again the microphone amplified the sound and a loud rasping noise crackled through the room.

"Hello, everyone," Daley said. "My name is Daley Marin. I'm running for president of the junior class."

Everyone's eyes stared dully back at her.

She cleared her throat. "Um, so I have a twelve-point program that I would like to outline for you, which will explain why I am the best candidate for this position. Point number one . . ."

She began talking about the towels in the locker room. Her theory had been that she should start with something that would appeal to Nathan's core voters first and get that out of the way. But as soon as she began to speak, it just seemed like the most trivial, dumb, irrelevant thing she could possibly find to talk about. Towels? God!

Time seemed to stretch out like some giant

rubber band. She could feel sweat popping up all over her body.

"Point number three . . ."

People were yawning and rolling their eyes now. She noticed that Eric McGorrill had fallen asleep in the front row. His head kept nodding over and then suddenly it would jerk back up. People around him had started to snicker. She realized with horror that she had over-prepared, focusing on all this nitpicky stuff, when what she really should have done was—

"Point number seven . . ." Her speech even seemed mind-numbingly boring to *her* now. She could feel her voice droning on and on and on. But she didn't know what to do to spice things up. She was chained to the words on the page.

Behind her Dr. Shook cleared his throat. She looked over at him uncertainly. He tapped his watch. She glanced down at her own wrist. Oh no! She'd been droning on for sixteen minutes already and she still had five more points to go.

She rapidly ran through the last few points, then departed from the speech with one last pathetic appeal: "I just hope you'll see that I really, really want to be president and that I'll work really, really hard and I'm really, really . . . I'm really, really . . ." She felt a wave of panic sweep through her. "I promise! I'll work so hard. I'll work *so* hard."

She clamped her jaw shut, walked to her seat and sat down, and ran her hand through her hair. She noticed for the first time this huge snag sticking up on the side of her head. She'd been so preoccupied with her speech this morning that she'd forgotten to brush her hair. She just wanted to run away and cry.

But she'd already done that once in front of everybody, hadn't she? And once was enough. She sat rigid as a board while Dr. Shook introduced Nathan.

"Okay, guys, here's Nathan McHugh!"

Nathan hopped out of his chair, walked confidently to the podium, spread his arms, and grinned. "What's uuppppp, Hartwell?"

The crowd began to applaud thunderously.

"Nathan! Nathan! Nathan!" A cheer began over in the section where all the football players were sitting, then faded when Nathan raised his hand.

"Hey, look," Nathan said. "We all know Daley. She's focused and disciplined and everything. She's great. But being president of the class—it's about people." He paused. "And, guys—" He put a little hip-hop inflection in his voice, spread his arms again. "Y'all are my people!"

Everybody cheered.

I am so dead, Daley thought. *I am so totally dead.*

At lunch, Daley and Nathan sat side by side

outside the cafeteria selling raffle tickets. There was a steady stream of buyers. Apparently the story about their Dumpster-diving expedition to find the money had gotten around to every single student in the whole school—because every ticket sale seemed to be accompanied by a new joke about how Daley and Nathan smelled like garbage.

Daley was never all that good at taking jokes about herself. But today she just sat there like she was made of wood, a forced smile on her face, making change and handing out tickets and wishing school was over so she could just go home.

At least it was the last day of school. That way she wouldn't have to wander around school for weeks feeling like she had a big L tattooed on her forehead. *Loser, loser, loser.* What could possibly be worse?

Nathan, on the other hand, didn't seem the slightest bit nervous. He was laughing and joking with everybody that came by, bantering about funny names they could give the monkey if they won the raffle.

When the bell rang for the end of lunch, Daley counted the money.

"So what's our grand total?" Nathan said.

"It was a good day. Our total's twenty-eight hundred dollars," she said. "We're going to Palau and we'll still be able to donate five hundred to the zoo."

"Much as it pains me," he said, "I gotta admit this was a better idea than doing another stupid car wash."

There was a moment of silence and then Daley said, "Congratulations."

Nathan frowned, looked at her curiously. "For what?"

"You'll be a good class president, I'm sure," she said. She wondered if her tone of voice sounded as unconvincing to him as it did to her.

"Hey, it's not over yet."

"Yeah, it is," Daley said. "After that terrible speech I gave." She sighed and stuck out her hand. "I'm sorry it all got so weird."

Nathan shook her hand. "Hey, if I'd been in your shoes, I'm sure I'd have done the same thing."

They looked at each other for a moment, then Nathan said. "All right. See you at the closing assembly."

Dan Rosenthal typed up the forms and brought them to his supervisor, Mrs. D'Angelo.

Mrs. D'Angelo was on the phone. She was a large woman with long, gray hair and a lot of hippie jewelry. She gestured for Rosenthal to sit down, then kept talking and talking and talking on the phone, going on about all her plans for the weekend.

Finally she hung up and said, "What's up, Dan?"

Rosenthal put the forms on her desk. She put on

a pair of reading glasses and frowned.

"Hold on, hold on," she said. "You want to put this kid in juvie hall?"

He shrugged, tried to look all sincere and caring. "Hey, I've tried everything. But this is a very troubled young individual. He injured somebody quite grievously. I think he needs a wake-up call."

"It says in the police report they're not even sure who cut this guy."

"You know how police reports are."

She looked at him like, *No, I don't know.* But all she said was, "This Operation Second Chance program is one of the mayor's pet projects. It doesn't look good if we just go tossing these kids in jail. I mean, this young man still has a huge amount of promise. Look at these test scores! The kid's borderline genius."

"I know, I know. But his attitude is very negative. He's still going back to the 'hood. Still hanging. Against my express instructions."

"Apparently he's going back to go to some kind of church."

"Church? It's a hot rod shop masquerading as a church. The guy who runs it has gang ink from head to toe. My guess, the whole thing's some kind of tax scam or something."

"Be that as it may, he's not giving any discipline problems at school. And he's holding his own at the top private school in the city. Where's the problem?"

"The problem is, if this preacher—or whatever he is—doesn't snap out of this coma, Cody Jackson could well go down for a 187. I think he needs to be in juvie right now. If you'll just sign right there then I can—"

She cut him off. "Leave the papers with me. I'll think about it."

Rosenthal felt a wave of frustration wash through him. He was so close to nailing this kid, he could taste it.

He forced a smile. "Sure. Sounds great. I'd appreciate your guidance."

TWENTY-NINE

RULE TEN:
BE YOURSELF (AND YOU'LL ALWAYS BE A WINNER)

So. Rule Ten? Same as Rule One. Be yourself. I know it's cornball, but as long as you're true to yourself, you'll always be a winner.

"Okay, guys," Dr. Shook said, holding up his hands to the auditorium full of kids. "I know this is your second assembly for the day, and I know you're ready to get home and start your summer vacations. But we've got two things to do before you stampede out of here."

Kids were murmuring and jostling and joking. Nathan sat near the back with Taylor. He let his fingers drift over and rest on her leg. She pushed them away.

"Can't you think about something besides my legs?" she said.

"I was just—"

"*Shh!*" she said. "Dr. Shook's talking."

For the first time since he'd given the speech that morning, Nathan was feeling nervous. He just wanted to get it over with now. He felt pretty confident he was going to win—everybody had been telling him that all day. But still. It wasn't over till it was over.

"Quiet! Quiet!" Dr. Shook waved his hands again. "The camping club has a fun little event for us. I know everybody's eager to name the monkey. Joining us onstage is Ranger Mike from the LA Zoo." A weather-beaten man wearing a handlebar mustache and a safari outfit waved to the audience. A small monkey sat on his lap. There was some applause and hooting. "Ranger Mike is going to draw the winning ticket and find out who gets to name this cute little guy. But first, let's get the other business out of the way. We're going to announce the winners of the elections. Jim? Could you give me the results?"

The president of the graduating senior class stood and handed him a list. Nathan felt his leg jumping nervously up and down. Next to him Taylor was having a whispered conversation with Abby about what clothes they were going to take to Palau. Didn't she even care who won the elections?

Dr. Shook started with the rising seniors. Cheers erupted through the auditorium as the winners' names were announced. Then he doubled back to the results of the freshman class elections.

"For secretary-treasurer of the ninth grade, the winner is Gloria Kennedy." There were some tepid cheers.

Come on, come on, come on! Nathan was thinking.

It seemed to take forever to get to Nathan's class.

"And now for the rising juniors . . ." Dr. Shook paused and looked around the room. "Secretary-treasurer, Les Akins!" Nathan's foot was bobbing up and down uncontrollably. His heart was beating hard. "For vice president, our winner is Billy Wen!"

More applause.

"And now, the results for what might have been one of the most hard-fought and contentious class president races in the history of Hartwell School . . ." Dr. Shook paused, then set the list of winners on the podium. "Before we go on, I'd just like to congratulate both Daley Marin and Nathan McHugh. They went at each other pretty hard. There was, as you know, an honor council hearing. This was a gloves-off match. But you know what? Today I saw those two kids sitting next to each other, working hard to bring home the bacon so they could go on their eco-camping tour to Palau. Nathan? Daley? Could you stand up?" He motioned to the two students.

Nathan felt slightly faint as he stood.

"Big hand for these two kids who so strongly exemplify the spirit of the Hartwell School!"

The crowd applauded. Somebody that Nathan couldn't see started singing, "You look like a monkey . . . and you smell like one, too!"

There was more laughter and cheering.

"All right, all right, settle down!" Dr. Shook grinned and put on his reading glasses. "This was a close one. It came down to a difference of only ten votes!" Nathan could feel his hands trembling. He felt this silly grin sitting there on his face. Should he sit down now? Before he could decide, Dr. Shook spoke.

"And the new president of next year's junior class is . . . Daley Marin!"

Nathan blinked. He was still standing. He felt like everyone was staring at him. Only they weren't. They were looking at Daley.

He couldn't believe it. Daley! After the speech she gave today? It was impossible. There had to be a mistake. He slumped down in his chair. Next to him Taylor was still jabbering about clothes to Abby.

"Taylor," he said. "Taylor?"

Taylor turned around and looked at him. "What?" she said. "Did something happen?"

Daley couldn't believe it. For a second she just stood there feeling like there had been a mistake. Everybody was cheering and looking at her.

Dr. Shook motioned to her. "Daley. Daley, how about coming on up and helping Ranger Mike with the drawing. It'll be your first official act as president of the junior class."

Suddenly she felt it shoot through her like an arrow—the realization that she'd actually won. It wasn't a mistake!

"I won," she said incredulously. "I won!" She raised her hands in the air. "I won! I won!"

"Yes, Daley, I know," Dr. Shook said.

"Sorry. Sorry."

She walked up onto the stage feeling like she was floating, and approached the microphone. "Thanks, everybody. I'm truly humbled and want to thank Nathan for running such a hard campaign. I think it really made me perform to the best of my ability." She waved at Nathan. He was slumped down in his seat, wide-eyed and glum, looking like somebody had dropped a bomb on his house. He was looking at her, but he didn't acknowledge her at all. She almost felt sorry for him. Almost.

"Okay, Ranger Mike," she said. "I'm going to hold out this basket full of tickets. You just reach in and pull one out." She grinned at the audience. "And don't let that crazy monkey near my head!"

The kids in the audience laughed and cheered.

She held up the cardboard box full of tickets. Ranger Mike reached over and pulled one out and handed it to her.

"And the lucky person who gets to name the monkey is . . ."

THIRTY

After the assembly was over, Nathan sat there in his seat for minute. Then he turned to Taylor, who was *still* busy talking to Abby, and said, "Well, that really sucks."

"What does?" she said.

"I lost."

She looked disgusted. "Well, that can't be right. You need, like, a recount or something."

Nathan shook his head. "If I lost, I lost."

Taylor looked up at the stage. Some girl from the ninth grade was holding up the monkey that she had just named. "Oh, he's so cute!" Taylor said. She seemed to have totally lost interest in the election. "What did they name him?"

"Who cares?" Nathan said. "I lost!"

Taylor looked at her fingernails. She frowned

like she was thinking about whether she needed them manicured or not.

"Let's get out of here," Nathan said.

"Uh, well," she said. "Before you go . . ."

"What?"

She cocked her head to the side. "I guess there's no good time to do this. But while you're bumming anyway . . ."

Nathan frowned at her. "Huh?"

"You remember the guy I told you about? The one that's been doing my fashion videos?"

Nathan squinted at her. What was she getting at? He'd just lost the biggest race of his life, and she was talking about *fashion?*

"Well, anyway," Taylor went on, "he's just been really sweet to me. And I think I need to make some space for him in my life."

Nathan blinked. "Space? What are you talking about, Taylor?"

She cleared her throat. "I think I'd like to start seeing him."

She was obviously making some kind of joke. That video dude was like twenty-five years old.

"I'm sorry," she said. "That's why I did the thing for you in the honor council. I thought I should do something nice for you before I broke your poor little heart."

He kept staring at her. "Wait a minute. Wait a minute. You're serious? You're breaking up with me? Right now? In *assembly?*"

She shrugged. "Sorry!"

He couldn't believe it. Taylor was amazing. Breaking up with him in assembly!

"Palau's gonna be totally great though, huh?" she said brightly. Then she frowned. "You're not gonna get all weird, are you?"

Unbelievable. Un-freaking-believable. Well, he wasn't going to sit here and beg.

Nathan stood up and walked outside. Kids were running out the door of the school. He started to go get his books . . . but then he realized, *I don't have any books. It's vacation.*

He walked out the front door. Kids were rushing by him. Nobody stopped to say anything to him. Nobody seemed to even notice he was there. The sky was a cloudless blue and the air was a perfect eighty degrees. But so what? What good was nice weather when you were the world's biggest loser? No beautiful girlfriend, no student council office, no nothing. He was just like everybody else. Ordinary, plain, vanilla, invisible, nobody.

Forty-eight hours ago he'd said to himself that he was in the middle of the worst day of his life. But he'd been wrong.

This was the worst day of his life.

THIRTY-ONE

The next morning Dan Rosenthal jumped out of bed and checked his email before he'd even brushed his teeth or taken a shower.

There was an email from his boss, Mrs. D'Angelo. He clicked on it a little nervously. Was she going to buy it or not? He read the note:

Dan,

Looked over the file. Based on the police and school info, I really don't see any justification for sending this young man to juvenile detention. However, I know you are closer to the case and have spoken extensively with the parties involved, including police and the administrators at Hartwell. If you believe there is legitimate concern for the safety of those around Cody Jackson, then I'm willing to back your recommendation. The signed

*forms authorizing transfer of the young man from
foster care to the juvenile detention camp at Paso
Robles are on your desk.*

    Doris D'Angelo
    Senior Case Administrator

Jackson had all his things packed. Clothes,
toothbrush, toothpaste, comb, a couple of books
and magazines, a few tools.

Elaine said, "You ready?"

Jackson nodded.

They got in the car and started driving to LAX,
the Los Angeles International Airport, down on
the south side of town. Davion and Tre were in the
back seat making noise and thumping each other
with their Power Rangers.

Jackson was feeling sort of strange. But he
couldn't put his finger on what it was. Maybe it
was that stupid fight he'd gotten into with those
guys who were trying steal the cars. Big Jay was
still in the hospital. That was not good. Jackson
was worried about his friend. And the DA had
not made a decision yet about whether to dismiss
the charges against Jackson. Until that happened,
he could still go to juvie. And in just a few more
months he'd be seventeen—eligible for adult
prison.

He had a bad feeling about the whole thing. His
CDSS caseworker seemed to have it in for him.

Well, two weeks in an island paradise would help clear his head. Truth was, he wished he could go there and never come back. What was there to come back to, anyway?

"Jackson?" Elaine said. "You're sure quiet."

Jackson didn't say anything.

"Are you apprehensive about leaving LA?" she said. "Maybe feeling a little homesick already? Hey, it'll be fine."

If you only knew, Jackson thought. *I can't leave soon enough.*

Rosenthal pulled up in front of the Hartwell School, double parked in front of the administration offices, and walked briskly into the building.

"Dan Rosenthal, CDSS," he said, showing his badge to the plump woman at the front desk. "I need to see a student by the name of Jackson, Cody Jackson."

The woman looked at him strangely. "Maybe you need to talk to Dr. Shook, our headmaster."

"I can't wait around here all day," he said.

She made a call on her phone, and after a couple of minutes the principal or headmaster or whatever he was appeared in a doorway at the back of the room. He was a kind of hippie-looking guy with gray hair and low rise jeans, like he was about to try out for some rock band. Rosenthal explained what he needed and the headmaster said, "How about we go back to my office for a moment?"

The headmaster led him back to his office. It didn't seem like the sort of office you'd expect at a rich-kid private school. There was a big poster of Jimi Hendrix on the wall behind the desk and a Gibson Les Paul leaned against an amp in the corner.

They both sat and Dr. Shook said, "What can I do for you?"

"Like I was telling the lady out there, I need to see Cody Jackson."

Dr. Shook looked puzzled. Dan Rosenthal was not in the mood for a bunch of slowdown tactics from some glorified high school principal. He took out the custody papers and set them on Dr. Shook's desk. "It's all there. Now I'd appreciate it if you'd let me see the kid."

Dr. Shook opened the folder, scanned it.

"You're *arresting* him?" he said. "You're putting him in *jail*?"

"That's not the term we use for juveniles. We call it 'placement.' We're placing him in the youth detention facility at Paso Robles."

"What for?"

"It's all right there. He stabbed a minister."

Dr. Shook flipped through the papers until he found the police report. "From the way the report is written, it sounds like Jackson was the victim here."

Everybody was a freaking nitpicker. "Hey, look, Mr. Shook—"

The hippie-dippy principal smiled thinly. "*Doctor* Shook."

"Doctor, Mister, whatever. Just give me the kid."

Dr. Shook said, "Don't suppose you noticed how empty the parking lot is?"

Rosenthal gave him an even stare. "What's that got to do with anything?"

"Hartwell breaks for summer vacation three days before the city schools do. He's gone."

"You mean I drove all the way out here for nothing?"

Dr. Shook folded up the documents and handed them back to Rosenthal. "Great meeting you."

"All right, I guess I'll head over to his foster mother's."

"No, when I say he's gone, I mean he's *gone* gone."

Rosenthal slapped himself in the forehead. That stupid field trip! The kid was going to—what?—Hawaii or something? How could he have forgotten? "That's *today*?"

"That's today, Mr. Rosenthal." Dr. Shook looked at his watch. "His plane leaves in forty-seven minutes."

"From where?"

"LAX."

Rosenthal grabbed his folder and ran out the door, fumbling for his cell phone.

Daley was busy making sure everybody got their luggage checked and that their passports and tickets were in order. There was only one person who hadn't checked in yet.

Then she saw him walking across the huge atrium of the LAX terminal. Jackson. He was carrying one very small suitcase—more of a gym bag, actually. Taylor could have fit four of his bags in her suitcase.

"Hurry up!" she said. "It's almost time to go."

Jackson nodded.

"You don't have any weapons in there, do you?" she said.

A very small smile curled one side of his mouth for a moment. "Just a knife."

"You can't fly with a knife!" she said.

"Sure you can," Nathan said, coming up behind her. "Dad gave me a hunting knife for Christmas. It's not a problem as long as you check your luggage." He pulled a knife out his suitcase. "See?"

Daley looked around nervously. "Put that away!"

"Nice," Jackson said, pulling something out of his gym bag. It was the same wicked-looking knife she'd seen him carrying in the Art Annex. The handle was wrapped in duct tape. "I made it myself."

"You made that your*self?*" Nathan said. "Very cool!"

"Yeah, I work at this garage that's got lots of

metalworking equipment. I was going to carve this Samoan design in the handle with the tools they had in the sculpture studio at Hartwell. But I sort of got interrupted."

"You made this all by yourself?"

Jackson nodded. "Figured we might need a good knife while we're camping in Palau."

Daley saw a couple of LAPD officers only a few yards away. "Put those *away*!"

Nathan and Jackson looked at each other for a minute, smiled slightly, and put the knives away. Then they took their suitcases over to the baggage check area and placed them on the pile of bags being checked in.

Knives! Daley thought. *What use could they possibly have for a bunch of big, scary knives? It's not like we're going to be stranded on some desert island!*

Mrs. Goodman, the chaperone, clapped her hands. "Everybody? Everybody? Let's move on through the security gates now."

Jackson followed the group as they headed down the concourse to the gate. In front of him, Mrs. Goodman's phone rang. She answered it, then handed it to Jackson.

"Jackson, hey, bro, it's Big Jay," the voice on the other end said.

"Thank goodness!" Jackson felt relief flood

through him. He'd been afraid the big man might die. And all because of him. "Are you okay?"

"I'm good. Just lost a little blood."

"What's up?" Jackson was puzzled. How had he gotten hold of Mrs. Goodman?

"I called your school, they said to call this number," Big Jay said.

"Oh."

"Look, anyway, I got a call from that idiot caseworker of yours this morning. He's trying to arrest you and send you up to Paso Robles."

Jackson's heart sank. "But I didn't do anything."

"I told him that. Problem is, as long as the charges against you stand, he can send you to juvie anytime he wants. If we can get the charges kicked, you'll be okay."

"Okay."

"That could take months, though. Where you at?"

"LAX."

"Good. Get on that plane as quick as you can. Once you're airborne, you're safe."

"Okay."

"Keep your head low, bro."

"Thanks, Jay."

"It ain't nothing."

Jackson hung up and handed the phone to Mrs. Goodman.

"Everything okay, Jackson?" she said.

"Yeah," he said.

Rosenthal parked his car in the tow-away zone in front of LAX's Terminal 5, flashed his badge at the nearest LAPD officer, then ran into the terminal and headed straight toward security. There was a special line for law enforcement to pass through. He ran toward it.

The alarm went off as he ran through the metal detector.

"Hey, whoa, hold up!" yelled a very large security officer, blocking his way. "Need to see that badge."

Rosenthal handed his badge to the officer. The officer squinted at it. "Department of Social Services?"

"Could we get a move on?" Rosenthal said. "I've got a subject I need to place in custody and he's about to get on his plane."

"Department of Social *Services*?" the officer said again. "I don't know that you're authorized to enter here."

"Look, pal—"

The big officer's eyes widened. "Are you taking a tone with me, sir?"

Rosenthal did his best to act pleasant. Which was not easy. "Hey, look, no, it's just . . ."

A second security officer, the one that watched the scanner, said, "Uh, Mike, he has a weapon on him."

The big officer's head turned sharply toward Rosenthal, and he put his hand on his own pistol. "Sir? Mr. Rosenthal, please turn around slowly and put your hands on your head."

Rosenthal wanted to punch the guy in the face. But somehow he guessed that was not going to help him get this kid in custody.

"No problem, no problem," Rosenthal said. "We're all on the same team here."

"Flight 1298 to Guam," the ticketing agent's voice boomed out of a speaker on the ceiling of the terminal, "is now boarding from gate 54." They were flying to the Pacific island of Guam by commercial jet. From Guam they were going to split the group in half and fly on a pair of chartered propeller planes.

Jackson glanced nervously down the concourse, hoping he wouldn't see the face of his caseworker.

Mrs. Goodman stood up and clapped her hands. "Line up, everybody! Get your things."

Jackson quickly jumped up and headed to the front of the line, his heart thrumming nervously. Everybody else was clowning and laughing.

"You look a little nervous, Jackson," Mrs. Goodman said. "I'm not big on airplanes myself."

"I'm okay," Jackson said.

Mrs. Goodman led the line of kids up to the ticket agent, handed all the boarding passes to the agent. Jackson walked slowly down the inclined tunnel of the ramp that led to the plane. As he passed over the small gap between the plane and the ramp, all the bright sunshine leaking through, he felt suddenly like he'd passed into a new world. He'd never have admitted it to any of the other kids, but this was the first time he'd ever been on a plane. If it weren't for the thing with his caseworker, he'd be feeling pretty psyched.

He walked down the long aisle, found his seat, and looked out the window. For the first time in a long time he felt like there was nothing dragging him down, pulling him back, pressing on him. It was a strange feeling.

He grinned to himself.

After a minute one of the other kids sat down next to him. Eric something-or-other.

"What's up?" Eric said.

Jackson nodded.

The other kids were filtering into the plane. Eric nudged Jackson, pointed at a blond girl. "Check it out. Isn't she totally hot?"

Jackson shrugged. Taylor something-or-other. Not really his type.

"I *know*! Awesome!" Eric said. "You hear she just broke up with Nathan?"

"Nope."

Eric squirmed around in his seat like there was something he wanted to say, like he was waiting for Jackson to ask him something. He had this little smirk on his face. Finally, when Jackson didn't say anything, Eric went, "You want to know a secret?"

Jackson didn't, really. But that didn't seem to bother Eric.

"I actually made them break up," Eric said. "You know why?" He waited for a second then said, "Because I'm gonna hook up with her."

Lotsa luck, bro, Jackson thought. Girls like that never went out with guys like Eric.

The plane began backing away from the terminal. The ramp was still there like a tunnel into empty space.

Suddenly Eric said, "Whoa!"

"What?"

Eric pointed out the window. "Check that idiot out!"

A man was running down the ramp toward the plane, waving his arms.

It took Jackson a second to recognize him. It was Mr. Rosenthal. Oh no! Oh no, this was the worst.

But then Mr. Rosenthal reached the end of the ramp and wobbled on the edge, still waving his hands. Two men appeared behind him, security officers. They grabbed Mr. Rosenthal, yanked him backward, and all three men fell in a heap. Rosenthal finally stopped struggling, his face turned toward the airplane.

Jackson waved at the tiny figure on the runway. Rosenthal started yelling something. Yelling and yelling, his face red with fury.

"You know that guy?" Eric said.

"Nah," Jackson said.

"Dude looks like he's got some anger issues, huh?"

Jackson almost laughed.

The plane continued to back away from the terminal. Pretty soon Mr. Rosenthal and the ramp and the two security officers were gone.

The plane shuddered to a stop and for a moment didn't move. Did that mean something? Were they going back? Jackson's heart began to pound again. But then they began moving forward, turning into the taxiway.

"Welcome to Flight 1298," a voice said over the intercom. "This is Captain Elsberg. We're fifth in line for takeoff and should be airborne for Guam in about three minutes."

Eric started talking as the plane taxied slowly forward. He was saying something about posters and the election. Jackson wasn't really paying attention.

As the plane came around and stopped at the end of the runway, Jackson had another moment of nervousness. What if Mr. Rosenthal had convinced somebody to turn the plane around? But then the engines began spooling up into a high powerful shriek, and the plane shot forward, pressing Jackson back in his seat.

Eric was still talking.

Jackson took a deep breath, put the earpieces of his portable stereo in his ears, and let the music blot out Eric's voice. For a moment a smile played at the corners of his mouth. *Yeah! I'm a free man! This was the life!*

And then they were airborne.

Daley looked out the window as Los Angeles receded. She didn't like flying. People were meant to stay on the ground. She gripped the armrests tightly. What if the plane just suddenly fell out of the air?

But of course, the plane kept rising steadily and nothing happened.

Chill! she told herself. She took a few deep breaths and began to relax. Out the window the sun glinted off the Pacific Ocean, waves sparkling like the facets of a million diamonds. *What am I worrying about? These things never crash.*

THIRTY- TWO

Okay. So, my name's Nathan McHugh. I was gonna do this video for my summer project about the ten rules for how to get elected president of my class. But that kinda didn't work out.

Yesterday I was just totally bumming. All I had were problems. I thought nothing good would ever happen to me.

But you know what? I got up this morning and for some reason I was like, Hey, you can't just mope around forever. Today's a new day. I'm the same guy I was before I lost the election, right? Nothing wrong with that.

So the only rule that I got right in my other video was Rule One. Well, actually Rule One and Rule Ten were the same thing. Be yourself. Even if you lose, you still have to be yourself, right?

So now I've got a whole new idea for my summer project. This one's totally killer! I'm going to do a video about my trip to Palau. I mean, why look back at all your problems when you're about to do the coolest thing ever? Starting in about fifteen hours, it's gonna be long white beaches and wild jungles and all these amazing animals and plants. Time for a whole new attitude.

Bring on Palau, baby! All my problems are over!

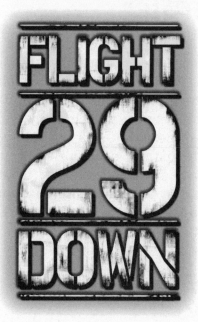

Read all of the books in this
action-packed series!

#1 Static

Flight 29 DWN has gone down, crash landed, and seven of its survivors—Daley, Nathan, Melissa, Taylor, Lex, Eric, and Jackson—have no idea where they are. They don't know if rescue is coming, or if or when their pilot and his makeshift search party will ever return. They were on their way to a school-sponsored eco-tour when the plane's engine gave out, and they're lucky to even be alive. But with food, water, and shelter being scarce, they're going to have to learn to put their differences aside and work together—before their luck runs out . . .

#2 The Seven

The stranded passengers of Flight 29 DWN have managed to survive for several days on a deserted tropical island—but they're beginning to wonder if they'll ever be rescued. Luckily, the castaways have honed their survival skills, and they're finding food to eat—however unappetizing it may be. But when personalities clash, fights ensue, and some serious crushes emerge, things *really* start to get interesting. Will the seven be able to stick together to make it until rescue comes—if it ever does?

#3 The Return

It's been a week since Flight 29 DWN crash-landed on a deserted island. Despite the occasional disagreement, the seven survivors are finally getting into a routine—until they discover that they are not alone. Will this mystery guest be the answer to all of their problems—or a disruption to the balance they've worked so hard to find?

#4 The Storm

The seven survivors of Flight 29 DWN have learned to trust each other for survival. But one of the passengers has a dark secret. And when all of their video diaries go missing, that secret may be unleashed, with drastic consequences ...

#5 Scratch

A storm has destroyed the camp—the food supply has been flooded, many tools are lost, and the boys' tent is in shreds. Jackson and his motley crew are going to have to start from scratch. But there's mutiny afoot as the group splinters off and teamwork dissolves. It's up to Jackson to keep everyone together—but can he handle the pressure?